Simon Brian Brewster was born in Bedfordshire, England in March 1976. At the age of eight years he moved to the west of Ireland with his family.

He was educated in Galway, where he wrote, partied and played rugby. At eighteen years he returned to England to attend university, but he did not complete his degree. Thereafter, for a number of years he worked on the continent.

Simon returned to Ireland, where he died in November 2002.

Simon Brewster

# START!

A NOVEL

Matador
9 De Montfort Mews
Leicester LE1 7FW, UK
Tel: (+44) 116 255 9311 / 9312
Email: books@troubador.co.uk
Web: www.troubador.co.uk/matador

ISBN 1 904744 90 7

Cover illustration: © Photos.com / Troubador

Typeset in 11pt Plantin Light by Troubador Publishing Ltd, Leicester, UK
Printed by The Cromwell Press Ltd, Trowbridge, Wilts, UK

Matador is an imprint of Troubador Publishing

For Nb
+
Kim

# Preface

It is the narrator's job in any work of fiction to present the facts as independently as he or she can and in these heady days of pragmatic confusion and optimistic bewilderment, stuck as we are on the cusp of a new era faithfully promised us by history, tradition and our own superlative beliefs, it is each persons right – nay responsibility – to detach themselves from these facts, to check their emotions and to hopefully logically and thoughtfully listen as the story unfolds.

For the time for panic has been and gone. The pressure of the establishment is dissipated and, alongside it, the church is being dismantled postulate by postulate – its wrong-doings and cover-ups unable to keep speed with its hypocrisy. To be sure, the extremists and fundamentalists remain, but all the rest of us can do is wait patiently for them to catch up. Those of you who have grasped freedom will appreciate the value of another's tolerance.

But of the here and today, patronized as we are by con-men high in self esteem and well-versed in their practiced poses, it is no longer a question of nihilism, of futile destruction, nor of a progressive anarchist utopia, but instead one of discerning taste. To acknowledge the effects of the politician and understand their effect upon the quotidian. There are few charges so grievous in the civilised and everyday as to be life-threatening, yet knowledge of the constraints the minority places upon the majority, and the willing abidance of the many to the few, can help us judge a nation's character, its strength and courage. Similarly, the people's manner of protest can help us measure its level of bourgeois naivety.

It is without ego that the narrator asks you to become complicit in his intent. For it is nothing more than an additional attempt to enter the annals of history, to tie myself to that particular masculine pursuit of killing time and hopefully, in the process, to understand the peculiarities of the multiple aspects, that determine the self, which ultimately realizes the individual. Little else can I ask of my audience. And so, dear reader, with a-drums a-crashing, and a-trumpets a-fanfaring and without further ado, can I present to you, the sweet, soulful tale of Jeremy S?

*"Lust for life"*
Albert Camus
*The myth of Sisyphus*

# 1

Now, Jeremy S, like Henry Miller and every other American in the world was a little retarded! There he was, stood by the carousel, nervously tapping his foot and watching, under the guise of patience as the bags flowed past. His arrival in the Capitol Airport of the Free State republic, had been understated, politely mingling with the other passengers, now banked around him in a congregated mass of common, controlled turmoil.

Some behind-the-scenes commotion had mixed-up the baggage, causing the Arrivals hall to be a disgruntled heave of travelers, while a plaintive woman's voice offered sincere apologies on behalf of the airline. But these problems little affected S. His mind lay elsewhere. It lay with the baggage handlers and the custom officers and his own fleet of foot. At any second now, his black, sports shoulder-bag would push through the flaps, driven slowly by the lumbering luggage machine – sail its way past the grouped onlookers and into his grasp. When that moment came, he'd have to pick it up and run with it. Behind him, someone shoved his back to get a better view. S twisted his neck and turned his face, moaningly breathing, as he felt his heart beat palpitations. As ever in an airport, time moved squarely, but his heart followed his head, leading to strained frustration, as he failed to even it out, the bag will arrive in its own way. He thought he glimpsed it once or twice, a shoulder strap here, a front face there, each time, his heart forcing the air through his mouth, giving him a short start or dive.

Finally, he spotted it and waited agonizingly as it made its slow passage – the silver logo tantalizing him as he pictured the other passengers picking it up. Some mistake or bitter spite, but no, he grabbed the strap and slung it onto his back and began manoeuvering his way through the mass. In the embattled rush, he followed the aura of confusion. The thronging crowds of tourists and holiday makers with heavy luggage and wonky trolley carts made it easy. As he spied the exit, giving him a choice of one of three, he casually checked them all out; meandering past the frequent flyers and nervous debutantes, while surreptiously glancing down the green channel before turning quickly away from the red and commandingly marching through the blue, the one reserved specially for EU citizens. Two uniformed officers stood there sharing a laugh and a joke. S breezed by.

Outside, he reached the cutting edge of the airport perimeter, the grass safely stashed at the bottom of his bag and felt his speeding blood subside and his heart's rhythm come back in tune. Now he felt somewhere between a self satisfied smile or regular demeanour, shuffling naturally as he waited for the bus to take him to the station.

At the capital's Lime Street station, Jeremy checked the billboard that timed the departures. Banks of TV sets to both his left and right screened 24 hours Sky news. The newsreaders crisp voice undermined the air. Her straight presentation as she read the report, crackled the stations frequency. Under the announcements and over the noise of screeching trains, she intoned the outbreak of war and ethnic cleansing in the Balkans republic of Kalarosva. Jeremy heard fractured pieces:

"...herding the people out... economic crises in the central... Pan Slavic Jews persecuted and... refugees along the Montenegron border...."

Jeremy idled about, sipping at coffee and waiting for the carriages to be cleaned. He joined a queue and slowly moved aboard, studiously finding a seat. He sat arranging himself, feeling the train quake as it began departing, the last passenger on board and heading his way.

"This seat is not taken, no?" asked the passenger.

"No" said Jeremy.

"Ah good. Such a rush you know. To negotiate the system. I struggle sometimes. Are you a tourist too?" asked the stranger sitting opposite.

"Of sorts" replied Jeremy.

"Oh yes. It is a fantastic country. So clean, so fresh. I am going to the west coast, yes? The scenery, it is splendid there? Beautiful, yes? You have seen it?"

"Ummm" replied Jeremy.

"And how far are you going?"

"To Oranmore."

"Ah yes, the last great outpost, or so they tell me."

"It's what they say. But it's not a holiday. More of a return."

The stranger opposite looked at him, through his spectacles, momentarily stroking his beard. "I am," he said "a dentist from Vienna. I was born and reared there, yet I often leave the country. To be sure, I love my land but I was raised elsewhere. And when I was a young man, I made a journey home, back to the splendour of Viennese living."

A little surprised at the old man's earnest revelations, Jeremy looked on ponderously.

"I saw great change there. A glorious oncoming of mobility and technology. I was very much taken with it. And I saw as I visited..."

"...around"

"Yes, as I visited around. I saw that the people, they had changed also. I visit friends and family and I see that they moved with the... technology, with the machines. And so I saw my brothers, my grandfather. And so, there we were, one old man, one young man, talking and we were best friends, ja? And every day this old man used to go to the park. An old whirling Viennese park in the suburbs and he would make his sandwiches and every day he would bring his sandwiches to the park. And at the park he would sit on this one old bench, the same bench every day, always the same bench, yes? And from that bench, there was a tree like this, yes?" The dentist moved his hands in an indicatory crossover motion, one hand moving past the other at perpendicular, parallel angles.

"Ja, and when evening fell, and they switched the electricity on, from the tree would come rodents, running down the bark, like little mice on their little feet and come up to my grandfather. And everyday he would feed them his sandwiches. Every day, they come down, every day he feed them, always at the exact moment. And he was so excited by the attention, the squeaks and the look in their eyes, ja, that he, himself looked young again. He said they were a new breed, new type of rodent. This kept him happy. It was his discovery and he wanted to keep it. He didn't show any others. It was his secret. It gave him fruitful youth and up until the day he died, he kept his secret with him. The new breed. Every day he would go to the park and feed the long tailed squirrels. Until the day he died!"

With slow precision, Jeremy looked out the window, night had fallen.

## 2

At the city of Oranmore, Jeremy got off to look for shelter. In control, round a corner and down an alleyway was Marcus Gondys' apartment, sitting atop a laneway, overlooking a bottle-strewn lawn. CCTV watched from the two ends as Jeremy crept along. He needed somewhere to stay and Gondys' was the closest in town.

He was surprised to see him, under the dim light, a smartly dressed spliff already in hand.

"Well welcome," Gondy said. "And how is the weather in London?"

"Fine. Can I come in?"

"But of course." Inside Gondy led him to the fireside, sat him down and immediately offered him a glass of wine.

"A fine claret" said Jeremy sniffing the air, a lingering waft of smoke catching him in the eye.

"An even finer spliff" said Marcus, ungraciously not passing it over. S produced the grass, laying the bags on the table. With a look of admiration under his spectacles, Marcus fed his hamster, the fireplace flames blazed up into his eyes.

"That's a swell haul. Gee it almost makes me wish I

had been with you, warding off swashbuckling demons at the gate."

"It was amazing stuff," smiled Jeremy. "Um quite. The stuff myths are made of." Jeremy had returned from abroad, in a mix of euphoria and delusion. Ecstatic with the smell of marijuana hanging over him. It had been a trip here and there, an exploration of the burden of South London roots.

"Conspiracy headquarters" interjected Marcus.

"What's that?"

"London" repeated Marcus. "Conspiracy headquarters. They'll know the day of apocalypse... the day before it happens."

"For sure."

"Yes, see, no matter the rest of information, the rest of the world may gather, London will always be blessed with one united knowledge. In all the planet there is only one sun!"

"For sure" said Jeremy.

It was attractive talk, he thought. London as the hubbub, the microwave centre of the world. Imagine...

"Sweet Mary and Joseph" said Jeremy. "What is that?" The crashing of the unlocked window in the wind sent a whistling sound spinning around the apartment.

"The wind is blowing its foul stink across this green and curvaceous town" said Marcus. Everything he said had a prophetic edge, a jitter of ominous intent. Jeremy, sitting across from him was nervous. Marcus kept his flat like a shrine; he invoked an unfocused atmosphere, heavy-topped and dense with strings of smoke, in which he shrouded himself from the slim light.

Jeremy, edgy, glanced surreptitiously at the speaker set-up.

Marcus smiled. "You like it, yeah! Picked it up through underground sources. I must say though, that it's absolutely immense for the price I paid for it. Pity I had to smuggle it in. That's the problem with this place, that bloody bank-sponsored Government tax on illegal imports. It's a complete farce."

Jeremy watched on as his compadre became more animated, the wind blowing through the chink, whistled through an oriental mystical chime, spookily intermingling with the glossy sound of Gondys' voice. Through the shroud, the revolutionary Marcus was underlining a melodious blueprint. "We are counterfoiled at every step by Government agents, those overinflated buffoons, sitting in judgement, passing down judgement, doling out punishment. Every invidious step they take consigns us ever deeper into their web... fuels paranoia, resentment... all to fatten their own pocket lining."

Glinting, Jeremy eyed Marcus. The stillness of the chimes was eerie amongst the strings of smoke, the weaving fireplace sending shadows flickering. But Marcus continued, his even, level voice, gently prodding the surreal atmosphere. Jeremy sniffed. "Hardcore" he mumbled.

"No doubt, yet I fear that come the day of reckoning, it won't be just them. It shall be strange souls like ourselves, like you and I. The dysfunctional reflection of their blinkered policies and virtues. For sure, the people are nothing if not a mirror image of its Government."

Marcus rolled another spliff. Jeremy sat, smoking

cigarettes with Actron filters.

"Can I sleep here tonight?" he asked.

"Of course. There is a comforting fold-out over there. And I will get you some sheets and pillows." The clock bonged and Jeremy checked his watch. The shock of the bells illuminated his dial. Almost precisely, his mind switched to thoughts of work, the rush of blood to his pineal gland, shooting him through with current-waves.

"Membrane liquefies" said Marcus, "with the smoke. The urgency of the bomblast is not lost with the consideration, the chronologically rationalism of things."

"Um" said Jeremy.

"Tell me, are you looking for money?"

"Yes!" said Jeremy.

"There is actually an interesting progression in this town at the moment. A new chap has arrived. A Sheffield fellow, by the name of Ove Arup. Employing a hell of a lot of people. You should go see him."

"Yes I will."

Marcus settled back and lit the joint.

"Where can I find him?" said Jeremy.

"He runs a club... the Third Eye Foundation, on Setanta Street."

# 3

The Foundation was run on a synchronized scale, its sequencing stemming from Arup at the centre and everything blossoming outwards. A seven-level set-up. It was the marble-stone of Arup's enterprise. One of a selection, a small-scale franchise, coupled on a legitimate footing. From inside, Arup doled out recreational drugs—upstairs, a state-of-the-art, fully functional, advertising friendly nightclub. Jeremy arrived at the bar with a saunter, the dancefloor livening up and the night ready to explode with the boombast sound of the drum and the bass.

One or two faces floated, Jeremy's memory recall was not acting on a glimmer of recognition, took his drink and moved towards Gondy.

Gondy was sweating a little under the lights, the netweb of strobes.

"Difficult to tell what floor Arup will be on."

They scanned the perimeter, moved up a flight or two, caught the eyes of two girls.

"Who are you?" asked Jeremy.

"I'm Suzie Q." said one.

"I'm Jessica" said the other.

"Glad to meet you Suzie Q, Jessica."

Q was petite and blonde with a vixen's face under a shower of curls, topped with startling faun eyes.

"I'm in marketing" said Suzie Q.

Under the subtle sophistication of the Foundation's interior décor, Jeremy sold himself well.

"And yet it won't be fire and brimstone that'll rain down" continued Marcus. "It'll be concrete degeneracy. Urban citizens will rise up with splits in hand and we'll seize our day in court."

Jessica, a bright young thing, looked on with reserved awe. Marcus gesticulated smoothly, intently, the jabs and articulation blending nicely with the atmospheric reverb. "I have no doubt, it'll be televised" he finished.

Isn't it awful, what's happening in Kalorosva?" said Jessica. They were partying in the glare of onrushing war. Troops were being readied, forces mobilised. Every day, more and more disappeared from the streets of Schrovny. Resistance forces were reported to be forming. An on scale battle was looming.

Jeremy and Suzie were getting it on. Jeremy had charmed her into his arms, the light reflecting upon his devils haircut. He talked seductively as she wriggled to his rhythm. Beyond, the club was panning out. Punters and groups immobilised under the disco beams, ecstatically eager, some almost panting with excitement. A steady flow of uniformed bouncers kept a constant watch on the stream of clubbers. Unseen faces adjusted unseen cameras, dissolving pictures, focusing lenses. Arup walked unhindered through the floor, his henchmen at his heel.

The foundation had formed from the ashes of Bassline boogie, a mildewing disco and cinema hall showing discerning art-house flicks for the elderly goer and pumping seventies sounds and soul into the basement downstairs. Arup built up. An entrepreneurial business-man, he'd left the vice in middle England. Closed his brothels when they fell into disrepute, traded estate and property. Bought three clubs in the Free-state and flourished. He was one of the old school that formed the new breed of damaged young market boys. An ace in manipulation, dealing schlock and profit.

The Foundation had a respectful footing. An innovative nightclub during the day, at night it crackled with the sale of illicit substances. All of Arup's political oeuvre tingled with the scent of stale marijuana. With a stroke of Dutch panache, he'd introduced the green, the streets and lanes already smoking the black. But in the blackwoods economy of the free-state tiger, prices had inflated, tablets became available to the highest bidder. The solid was smoked and choked and chaos reigned in the consumer department where knives and bats were often produced. Arup kept within context, reasonable drugs at reasonable prices but had to contend with outside forces – the reams of youths and youngsters, manic on amphetamines, swallowing smack and strychnine but each making a buck or two in the format. Arup industries, to thrive, had to police itself in a dog eat dog world.

# 4

Melissa was on her way home, across the campus at night. She was returning from the Federation of communists, social association, when she was mugged by two youths. They had waited, hidden by the bushes for communist members to pass by. Often they would just jump out and attack, creating havoc, this new age of hoodlum doctors, terrorising their patientless victims. Here they demanded her cash, her watch, her jewellery and maintained they had a weapon.

She froze.

"Gimme your money" they said.

She turned and ran. Through the billowing but vacuous campus, she fled – the youths in pursuit, snarling at her heels. She screamed. The closed-circuit camera watched her movement and her pursuers chase. It caught their momentary gain and their cowardice when the security officer appeared. "Hoodlums" soothed the officer, "just goddamn hoodlums."

Melissa was shaken and wanted to recover. They returned to the watchroom, to call the police, to catch a little air and maybe to have a cup of tea. "Welcome to the bizarre, paranormal world of the security officer," he said, as he opened the door to his little kingdom.

"Terrence is my name, and this here," he said, is Elieas Vaughan." He pointed to a stoop fellow, with shifty eyes, sitting in front of a monitor screen.

"Pleased to meet you ma'am."

Melissa smiled and Terrence sat her down, offered her coffee and made her relax.

"You shoulda seen me, Elieas," he said. "I was like Mr. Mojo rising himself, coming outta that night. Them two young fellows didn't see a goddamn thing, until I took it atop o' them. By crikey, they won't forget me in a hurry."

"You didn't catch them though, didya Terry? Got the whole thing on tape, ma'am, every invidious little shot, all the side steps, the grainy intrusions. You ever see that? You should see that sometime. Brings it all to another dimension. When we capture the scum for real."

"Point blank, so to speak."

"Point blank!"

Melissa watched as the two talked, snug between the altercating camera faces and the surreal calm of the officers' conversation. Protected, she steadied herself from the brunt of the attack. See, even under the neon strung façade at the heart of Oranmore, it wasn't all jazz cafes and beat-nik lighting. The spiraling drugs feud was afflicting all. Downtown joints and sidebars were getting splayed. The heat was coming down heavy and the busts were large. The Frankie Five Fingers, the saloon, both shut down. The Atomic Brown café under constant surveillance. It wasn't a pretty city. Packs and gangs were numerous.

"We pick up a good many of them trying to sneak in here. Giving me their schtich. Well, I'm Mr. Mojo..." Melissa watched as Elieas Vaughan operated the cameras and Terrence droned. The sprawling university grounds stretched through the town's laneways and thorough-fares, all covered by long distance television and Vaughan and Terrence observed a retinus flow of comers and goers, the pack-like persona evident in all, formulated by students particularly susceptible to bouts of madness and individual renegades, laughing hysterically as if driving funny upon a twilight motorway. Images flashed up. Drunk and doped youths spitting, fighting, rucking and urinating. There on the myriad of screens and monitors, insanity was unfolding. People were reaching back, uncaging the animal within and giving birth to beasts with eyes emerging before and behind. The two officers watched passively. Mute reflections in the televisual gaze.

ભ૯૪ઝ

In the Atomic Brown café, guests hopped to and fro, to a funky monkey rhythm with the crescendo of saxophone and symbols rushing to the top. There was timid laughter at the notion of surveillance. Deals were done openly, few busts made, yet the rumours continued. Arup in a bid for ever-widening supremacy and with snoot cocked made a bid for the place. Turned down upon the grounds of unfavourable character, but the real reason, more than likely was the "us and them" mentality, fostered by the locals, against the enterprise and outsider dealing. Rather, the small unorganised knife merchants than sleek, informed business management. Brooding hostility was bred here. Bred and nurtured.

The Atomic Brown lacked charisma. The floating music and pretty waitresses obliged, easy on the eye but its moments of stealth collided with an unseen vulgarity. Drunken, stoned youths sickened upon Teflon seating, like old men and women, stuck in the last throes of an hallucinogenic death. Gasping for air, violently retching, they filled all the tables, swapping shady narcotics under the counter, hollering and wailing, like cattle to the slaughter. Jeremy and Marcus arrived, ordered their fusioned drinks and took stools.

"Spiritually, they are dead," said Marcus, fondling his cigarette.

"Yes how so?" replied Jeremy.

"That zest is missing. You know. Now it is more like succumbing to all that is so dry. It's a bloody morass out there, every day, day after day, in which we all struggle and fight. But these zombies suck up that cathode ray without contrast."

"They've started dropping bombs. Fighters over the Balkans."

"Well, I'll be damned... Oh and by the way, Arup has work available. I heard it from a good man. I do believe he's raising the stakes somewhat."

# 5

Arup was branching out. Finally sickened by the hostile forces, Arup was going to eradicate the enemy. In a plan of cunning, Arup was ready to flood the market with the purest ecstacy. No more of those speckled riddled pills, and the extravagant money-merchants who sold them. No more of the fear they caused.

But his benevolence masked the authoritarian power behind it. It he could cleanse a city like Oranmore, then a nationwide expansion seemed viable. He needed to build an army now. No longer any good his mish mash of lackeys and entourage, whom he easily controlled, while holding them under armed sedation. A pinch here, a swipe there – here's the j, g and check your head.

He wanted to build the Foundation like an agency. Well-dressed goons with shades ready to fight, to scrap and battle to eradicate the boot-boys. And he wanted couriers to smuggle and to smuggle honestly.

Now, he swung on his swivel chair in the shadowy confines of the management suite of the Foundation. Power and glory were flooding through him and yet, as he clenched his fist, something growing inside his mind ticked over. Henchmen were scattered, waiting nervous-

ly for him to speak. Their yelping subsided, the silent air
disturbing them and Arup, one hand on his bloated
stomach, an imposing presence. With a cyborg's vision,
he scanned each one, a half shut eye, taking in detail,
reading features, noticing each shiver and chill, as his
troops braced themselves. I need new people, he
thought.

"Alright, everybody except Andrews, get out!"

The countryside drug dealers marched out, only
too happy to be released. Arup rose their blood, sitting
quietly like that. Rose their fear of an institutional education, a beating from the men in white coats.

"Andrews, I want fresh faces. I have to recruit new
staff – at least four. Dependable fellows, I can count on
in my hour of need. Do you understand? No more of
these weak-willed.... Find me some men, Andrews."

Andrews nodded.

Andrews was Gondys contact. After a couple of
phonecalls and promises, Jeremy and Andrews met.

"You'll have heard of Mister Arup" said Andrews.

"Of course," replied Jeremy.

"Well Mister Arup is expanding."

They entered the Foundations sanctum, into the
back, shadowy office of Andrews, a bug-eyed servant of
some stature. He was Arup's hand-man. Tall and lank
and moist with the sleazy veneer of a nightclub, styled
in a sharp-cut suit, pin-stripe tie, left loose at the neck
and topped with straight greasy hair, he was a twee man
in middle management.

"Right, the Third Eye Foundation is here, this
building and we have five more throughout the country,

all operating under this umbrella superclub. Aha, sure! This is Mister Arup's base but he's relocating, possibly abroad, where he hopes also, to become economically involved. Do you understand!!" demanded Andrews.

"Sure," replied Jeremy, recoiling from the defective transmission line.

"The Third Eye" continued Andrews intently, "is an extremely viable proposition with frequent career opportunities. We may only have an opening on the club floor, or in the party group, but progress and promotion are frequent and varied. Capiche?"

"Yes."

"So, what... what are you looking for?"

Jeremy explained. Low cost, low quality income, with few questions and flexible hours. Andrews stared, Jeremy stared back.

"Some of the work may come with a little risk. Would you be prepared for that?"

"Without a shadow of a doubt."

"Right, let me give you the guided tour."

With a gauche lollop, Jeremy followed him to the exterior. "All this," said Andrews, "from top to bottom is pure. It's all clean. This is all Arup's, yes?"

"Sure."

"Six dance floors, one basement, one management suite. There are four bars. Should we employ you, you'll probably be in management. Be on that payroll and you're sussed. D'ya know what I mean?"

Jeremy swelled with distinctive irony. Indistinctly, he agreed. The chaos on the streets had released a surge of emotion. Awful epidemics were emerging, that were slaying strings of stricken junkies. The holes and cracks in the fabric were lengthening, the divide growing greater. The sanctuary of the inner suite, would present sweet respite.

They toured the club together, exploring its metallic façade. Indubitably, a pulsating heart throb through the entertainment sector of the West Coast, the Foundation was a money-weaver. It produced cash hand over fist, night after night. The others, though lacking in hands-on care, flourished. The free state had been conquered, the banks easily tamed. The future was rushing on, no longer head bound in collision.

"But staff, staff are a problem. Right, let me give you my card-here-I have your number. You will call me! Yes! We will talk more."

"Okay," said Jeremy, taking the card with honour.

"Okay, let's go."

Down they went. At the doorway, Andrews said his goodbye and Jeremy went his way. To Gondys, backwards past the bells of the church he went. A thick mist lay across the land and he wanted off these streets.

He was welcomed warmly by Gondys fireside, the flames searing their eyes, whiskey scorching their throats.

"It's a good malt."

"Displays all the fine beauty of the Tao se Tung," considered Marcus, "but elegantly concealed."

In the corner of the room, the hamster spun around on its wheel, her eyes peeping at the ray of the cathode tube. 24 hours Sky News played continuously, pictures of war colluding with deep, rumbling sonars of bass.

Shudders of fear crossed between the walls and hearts beat fiercely.

"This is intriguing," said Marcus. "We are watching our own slow-burn descent into hell!"

The dissolving blue outline deceived Jeremy momentarily.

# 6

Arup was in pain. His stomach burnt and his face looked like a twisted churn of butter. Shooting pains of sensation shot through his back, as he bore the burden of his belly, his dreadful weal and woe that almost crippled him and left him paralysed in his chair. He grunted and groaned with discomfort as he adjusted himself, his heavy weight of growth, stunting his breath. Steadily he inhaled, while his exhalations came in short, quick gasps. He sucked on paracetemol for relief and his lardy frame shuddered with expectancy. On his desk, sheets of papers and notes scrambled for space, dotted with numerals, symbols and projections. Perceptively, he visualised this new growth as a retirement. No more battling from the front line, rather a cushy number in top-level management. A mini empire at his beck and call and jumping to every word he barked. But the pressure was intense. Enemies were going to be made and a lot of already angry people were going to be upset. He moaned with movement as his belly rumbled at the alien awakening.

The metaphysical persuasion was not foreign to him. Already he spent his days as a balding uberbaby, away from the glare of others and their piercing looks that demanded something, the violent demand to be saved and taught. Now, even expeditions outside were fraught with danger while the packs roamed armed with sticks and the dull sheen of their yellow teeth, ready to stalk at the drop of a hat. Saliva and drool flew through the air as they ranted and raved. It is no wonder I am suffering like this, he thought, while the nihilists run the social asylum. With a loud belch, he summoned Andrews in via the intercom.

"Andrews," he said. "Don't toy with me. Tell me you have found some men."

"I have two of the four," answered Andrews. "Jeremy S and Nigel K. I believe we're making contact today."

Arup looked on in silence, his face bent and his eyes peering upwards. "Two is fine," he said. "For now. I asked for four. I need four."

"Interviews are still ongoing, Mister Arup, sir. I am sure we will achieve the full quota."

"Work is proceeding, Andrews. I need men. You will, of course fully understand the implication of that statement."

"Yes Sir."

"Excellent. Now go!"

"Certainly."

For Andrews, it was second nature to navigate the complexities and intricacies of Arup's system. A loyal second in command for years, Andrews had watched as business grew and simultaneously as Arup's reclusiveness strengthened. Andrews had often commanded when Arup would lock himself away, either in his studio office or apartment flat, binging on alcohol and dope, surveying his empire from the sanctity of sofa or swivel chair. The times when he would cocoon himself away from the prying eyes of a hostile public. And these times ran smoothly under the guile of Andrews care. A soft-focus management style, where the ephemeral qualities shone and tricky kinks and twists were avoided. Silently, he shuffled the papers. Glanced at the CVs, marveling at the transitional details and moved on to contact names.

An appointment was scheduled for late afternoon. The smiling Jeremy and the pointed Nigel would meet.

At that moment, Melissa was leaving her home, a chill wind blowing through the metal garden railings. Under the steel-holding railway bridge towards the centre she walked. From the suburbs, the urban blast was exploding as she continued along graffiti adorned streets and pacing the scruffy sidewalks. The beckoning hum of life was alluring in the shadowy noon-tide. Here, she entered the realm, a selective tavern left of the Foundation, cold and electric with sophisticated vibrancy.

"You are welcome" said one, who stood and offered his stool. "Here take this."

With charmed efficiency, a drink was placed in front of her.

"It is a calming storm that is brewing today," said another. Smiling, Melissa agreed. The air was heavy with ominous intent, a magical edge cutting the ambient fear. In here, they moved in glacial angles, a pressurised motion in defence of their position. Slim and beautiful,

Melissa mixed easily.

"I hear you had some trouble," said one, sipping his drink precisely.

She told him about the attack and he listened intently. Afterwards he consoled, encouraged and cajoled.

"Ah, some are not so lucky, no?" They talked a little more, glad of the refuge from the apocalypse outside. Time sidled by in here, sheltered from the afternoon rain. A little bit later, she left and walked right past Jeremy as he entered the Foundation.

# 7

"Nigel, Jeremy... how the hell are you?" Arup greeted the two men with customary staunch, muttering through gritted teeth.

"Okay! Now we get down to business, I need men. Ones with stomach and fight. I'm running a tight ship, I'm line walking and I'll have no deals with that two bob police squad out there. What I'm looking for is dedication and courage. You get me? Tight mouths are an essential. I'll need protection, here, in the club and an athletic young man to run the borders. I'll put you on the payroll and you can start from there. For finances and further instructions, talk to Andrews. Now get the hell out!"

Arup burped loudly and the two departed.

# 8

It was in the general composite of the break-up of things that Jeremy and Nigel met. In the anteroom interior, they sat down and waited for Andrews.

"Where are you from?"

"Tokyo."

Jeremy nodded in affirmation. There had been jaunty surprise at the transitional ease, the townscape was infused with meditative revolt – though the cityscape was still littered with the dregs of rural renaissance. Someone had touched the under middle class with a zen like commodity of passive resistance.

"And you?"

"Nowhere."

"This is an exciting time. Now I shall come fully to terms with this standard of living. It is a peculiar phenomenon to me. To you too, eh, I expect?"

"The assimilation is of much interest."

"Yes yes. It is a peculiar experiment. Mister Arup thinks he is mercury, yah? A doctor of physics, no doubt and his way shall be one of madness."

Nigel mused on the myth of insanity. The shortfall could always be countered by the helium. Science would no doubt be the mean, but what price the justification?"

"You pay, how much you pay for this room?"

"Eighty."

"Eighty too small. Gimme eighty-five."

"I'll give you ninety without a deposit."

The property agent paused, then accepted. "Yeah, okay. You give me ninety and you can have it."

Jeremy counted the cash out, handed over the wad and took the key.

"Hope you have a very pleasant stay."

The empty shell of the flat was stark and affecting yet adequate. Few plans had yet been made for an official homecoming, so there was no necessity for intricate internal development. The walls were bare and whitewashed, though splashed with solar spots, increasing circles of black condensation. He arranged the room to his liking, its minimalist circumstance adding an abstract indolence. The only extravagance was the cable reaching to the socket at the back of the television set. It powered up. Jeremy began a leafy construction, the heavy grass low, lighting the heady reaches. On the television, he tuned the channel to the news. Digital focusing units flashed up photographs of the bombs dropping. Seedy, yet technical, black and white tape rolled, carrying pictures *shot from the underside* of an aircraft, before showing the mute explosion of white tinged destruction. Munition dumps, factories, libraries; all crumbling from a hail of Armageddon from the skies. The Governor of the EU, the president of the British Isles appeared on the screen. He gesticulated broadly in a split minute virtuoso performance.

Still more Pan-Slavic Jews were shepherded away from Kalarosva. Camps were being established. Rotten tents in lifeless fields were being erected. Charity funds appeals were designed and quickly forgotten, while Union troops mobilized in the capital, Schrovny. Around the city and surrounding towns, there were guerilla warfare occurrences and there were persistent, random reports of militia attacks and state army atrocities. The governor of the EU, the president of the British isles demanded an end to the violence.

"The struggle must stop," he said.

It was with detached loquacity that Jeremy watched the unfolding rumble. It was providential politics, leadership decisions based on chance. The methodical attacks had no real sequencing, merely the power of might as its support and the gentle televisual editing lessened the impact of the horror of the war. The digitally-enhanced satellite photos only lent an edge of autonomy to the robotic viewer, distance handled the rest.

# 10

The sky crackled with the hiss of expectancy, the air stiffening with electrical charge. Bolts of lightning jumped from cloud to thundery cloud. In the streets below, Jeremy bumped into Melissa. He slipped on the rain-swept sidewalk, his sole taken from beneath him.

"Oh my God, I'm so sorry. Are you ok?"

Jeremy brushed himself down. "Fine," he said. "I hope I didn't hurt you."

"No," said Melissa, "not at all," and smiled.

"It is a dangerous pavement," said Jeremy, "we should shelter from the sky." She went with him for coffee into Atomic Brown, where they took a booth. They talked smartly huddling closer as time went on.

"So what brings you here?" she asked.

Jeremy talked a while, stringing out sentences of scattered explanations. Truth was, he needed bearing. Anyway, he fell more easily, had no basis, no fixing, nor secret history. Here was the bottom of the abyss and he could sniff the other side.

Her eyes flashed green as he spoke, a born-again naturality evident in them. Around the couple, the café panned out, filling with customers, tittering nervously, aware as they were of their own thoughts, as of covert surveillance. A mounted plain-clothes operation, goons with cameras, perched in their vehicles, blindly staring at shadows alert in these teeming streets. Suddenly spooked, Jeremy sat ramrod straight.

"We should leave," he said quietly.

"It's raining."

"We can talk easier elsewhere. Come, it will only be a short walk."

Together they stepped out, into the rain, squeezing close for warmth.

"Everywhere, they listen" he said. "Everywhere you go, someone is reacting to something we have said." With an age-old caution, borne of solitary wisdom, Melissa looked up to the be-suited rebel, walking close beside her.

"We can discuss here, it's a pleasant tabernacle." They stood outside the Pied Cow, a quaint establishment, patronized by young and elderly locals. They took a table and Jeremy went to the counter. An ignoble bartender served him drinks and looked on dismissively. Ambling, Jeremy returned to the table, feeling the heat of the glare from the regulars.

"The reception is frosty."

"They're okay. They're just not used to change. It's a difficult progress."

Regulars sat in bubbles, croakingly gasping for oxygen. The unrest and perpetual motion was unsettling for them. Trepidation haunted these streets and lanes at night, and even the short days offered little solace from havoc wreakers shattering the calm. Reaction after action spread like wildfire, the bank sponsored community, warily confused from lack of guidance. Media sections were monopolized in a vain attempt at seductive reasoning, but to no avail; its content not contending with diverging social reality. In fact, it misled, backfired even. It hailed the councilman as saviour and promised blessed relief to an unexpecting public. Now, the miserly back line was right in control, yet missing countless opportunties. Chaos spiralled and an independent vanguard emerged, a minority of individuals prepared to lead a life on principle.

"I am an anarchist" said Jeremy.

"That's ok," soothed Melissa. "You know," she said with coy complexity, "I'm a party member."

Jeremy was taken aback. It was an unexpected shock. "Still?!? Even now?"

"Yes! Even now!" Melissa was a vehement supporter of the rights of the party and the right to belong.

"The party is tolerated?" asked Jeremy.

"We are accepted..."

"...but not assimilated, no?"

"No I find it comforting, though. There is a sense of order, of soriety."

"Soriety?" questioned Jeremy.

"It is primarily girls... women, as members. There are two ugly men there, but they hardly talk and we rarely fraternize." Jeremy looked into her eyes. They were still with the urgency of life and a sense of ease. For you, he thought, I would sacrifice myself! Tenderly, he took her hand atop the table. He felt the urge to protect her, over the coming days and weeks. Instinctively, he would offer assurance, sanctify their position and vend off intruders, so dazzled by her sexuality, latent or not, was he.

"I've begun work at the Foundation," he told her.

She looked on with a sexy smile. It was only now she was becoming alive to the possibilities... A fatal mistake had brought them here today, that was never in the scheme of things... but one which oozed with sensuous potential...

# 11

"...Well goodbye, then."

"Yes, goodbye."

They parted at Melissa's front door. A gentle kiss and he was gone, an intricate spell working upon him. The sweet smoothness of his head kept him cool, but this meeting had revived his desire. The apathetic fight was attractive in its insousiance, but this adrenaline rush of passion left him alive with energy. Earnestly, he walked home, dodging the lights and ducking the traffic, a flameswell of opinion spacing on him and projected through the ether into the hazy static of neon-lit compartments and purple fascias.

Later, spliffed up in the Foundation, Jeremy sauntered through the club, checking the lay of the land under low-level lighting. Four men had been recruited to secure Mister Arup's future and Jeremy was handed cross-border runner. Previously, Arup's former lackeys had been cast out from the management suite and were now roaming the floors, an uneasy jealousy brooding between them, the old vs. the new. And Jeremy, the outsider, had little more to do between runs, than hang around the club, like a pretty decoration and suck up their spite.

Moodily, he surveyed the scene. Somewhere betwixt kingdom and exile, he stood poised with an arrogant sneer, contending the enemy. The expelled henchboys were notorious cannibals, masking viciousness behind a giggling, drooling front. Veiled threats would come under the guise of a multitude of backward accents and accompanied by the grimace of a dead man. Every encounter was two dead men together. He was spurred up by the attention of the Mexican, a volatile chapita blow-in with an angry line of chatter.

"You working for Arup now, my son?" taunted the black eyed Azteca, a few yards away.

S read his mind. 'Could you kill a man at fifty pesos?' thought the Mexican.

"For Arup!? Yeah I work for him."

"And what do you do then, sol boy? What do you work? You work the floor? You the trained monkey that gotta keep all the little boys and girls happy?" The Mexican laughed in his face.

"You ain't nothing, sul boy—"

The Mexican taunted the fowl in him. Grittily, Jeremy ignored the man, until finally he walked away.

"I get you again, soul-boy. I get you again."

Any anxiety subsided, the ease supported by the fact of the professional payroll. One of the appointed few, the exile slowly evolved. The floors were his, to watch over, to mind, to exploit and for a reasonable period, to judge... in penitence.

# 12

In the quintoxic palisades of Arup's office space, the four men lounged. Andrews stood to design, as casually motionless as Arup was behind his desk.

"Alright, men, listen up. This is day zero. From here on, this club goes clean. Not one spliff, one pill or one wrap of fuel shall be consumed here. We'll leave that to the other branches. Andrews, sit down."

"Yes okay."

"Right I am shutting down two floors to convert into offices. You four will be based here. As will I, for you to protect, except... you... Jeremy S. You will be exporting and importing to my timetable and under volition. You get caught, you squeal, you're dead. Okay?"

The ska-faced S looked on.

"Right now, the local fuzz along here know me. They couldn't fail not to, but they're bent. Completely and utterly. However, I can't get them into my pocket because of some twisted backward loyalty or other. So I don't want or need them. I don't want them in here. I want faces spotted, files made up. If these goons are making a move, I want to know about it first."

He stood up. "From all of you I expect complete dedication to my case. I can't ignore the cosmic rumblings that compel my intervention. There is a revolution being heralded by my presence and I am at the forefront of the new social order. You'll give me protection, be prepared to die for the cause, to fight for the cause, and in return, the cause will reward you well."

Andrews intervened. "You are now in Mister Arup's employ. We expect you know the rest. This is the major league, gentlemen. Any showings will be incognito, there will be few sudden movements and a vigilance to the job. You are the elite, the entourage will remain but they are disposable. They answer to your command, but, and I stress this, we want no antagonism, no displays of hedonistic glory. This is to be a smooth operation, expansion and merger. Thank you for your assistance. You may go."

The four men filed out, expressions muted, the stoney gravel of their features unalterable in the heat of Arup's blast. Now, perched along a bar, they took advantage of their new-found superiority. Drinks were served to the four men while people swept the floor and cleaned the glasses.

"We are kept souls now," said one.

"Rather that, than streetfighting battlers. We give protection, we earn a little," said another.

There was Jeremy and Nigel and two Italians sitting together. "You... you have it good, though," said an Italian, wildly gesturing towards Jeremy. "Travel for free, you get all the perks. Yes?"

"Ah, but I take all the risks."

"Ha ha, says he, with his pockets overflowing with gold."

"Okay gentlemen," interrupted Nigel. "We remain professional about this at all times. We are employees together. What you say, eh, eh?"

"Yes, yes, but of course," intoned an Italian, "but we can never forget that this is a highly intense business, amico."

"Arm us!" said the other.

Andrews had appeared, sliding through the nightclub air with gauche abstraction like a placid owl. He had perched upon the corner of the bar, grimly observant beneath his expensive designer suit.

"Arm us!" repeated the Italian to Andrews.

Andrews looked up. "The solicitous nature of the programme forbids this. However... this is a... shall we say, an illicit operation. We expect our employees to be able to fend for themselves. Remember, our location is served well by the passivity of the regulars. Life threatening it may be, life-endangering it is not."

Andrews finished his drink. "You have free rein gentlemen. I bid you goodnight."

## 13

—This is delta 454 zero requesting ground control clearance—

—Delta 454 zero, this is ground control, you have clearance take her in—

The airplane landed safely, the karma working through the wings, before Jeremy repeated his earlier charade in the airport. Security had been visibly stepped up and some uniformed officers were highly conspicuous. The ethical teachings of nature were lost in the airport hum, the social conventions of man powering up in this great perspex of glass and metal and fuel. The heightened presence of guards wasn't affecting as the ritual was repeated. Jeremy had undergone the inevitable inconvenience of being body searched, the foil in his cigarette packet, consistently setting off the alarms of the metal detectors and at each one he readied himself in sacrificial posture as the customs officers patted his frame down, checking all pockets for chemicals, weapons.

Once, he had stood behind a mouthy American, reluctant to send his camera film through the x-ray machine.

"We don't do this in America. It'll damage the film."

The customs officer refused to check it by hand.

"Through the machine please," he said.

"It'll damage it."

The American had complained loudly, his high-pitched protestations echoing the queue. People shifted uneasily at the scenario. The ugly spectre of "home-made" film was rearing its head in the departure lounge of a Netherlands airport. Jeremy followed the American, who had spread his arms in compliance, the Yank and the photo film, his reels of tape and its grainy imaging had safe passage back to his industry and the shock-horror effect and smile that blotted the network.

Always focused and ever-analytic, Jeremy waited under the penetrating gaze of the closed circuit lens, its eye processing the motion picture and its continuous movement, shape-changing through black and white alignment, being enhanced, clarified and coloured, until the finished image was flashed up on a screen else-where, to be dissected and dismembered by hard, unseen, sneering faces. Pressurised people coming on the unmerciless, thought Jeremy.

With the highly-charged air of militancy and terror-ism, fear and threat were imminent, yet under his chameleon-like lack of hair, the hidden surveillance of the video telemetry system was no burden. His incogni-to style was magnificent, doppelgangers were many and varied. S was able to blend in any crowd, unseen by enemy faces and with instinctive diffidence. He easily slipped by the cordon of the security, X amount of high quality pills in his luggage. The trip back to Oranmore was uneventful and left Jeremy to reflect silently on his protracted colour and experience. Every journey strengthened his resolve, teetering, as he was, on the edge of invincibility.

In the sticky exterior of the Third Eye he was welcomed and in the management suite he produced the ecstasy, at cost, on the level and justified by his own smuggling of the green.

Arup was indisposed, on the toilet, the three others guarding him attentively, offered relaxed congratulations as Jeremy revealed the haul to Andrews.

"Excellent," he said, matter-of-factly, taking the merchandise.

The club was geared for a hectic night. Jeremy and Melissa met up, and the music drummed on. They stood together as the crowds heaved, livid on pure e, the new range of cyber-punks dominating, while the elderly clubber remained in the shadows. Above inflated beats and the new sounds of staccato rhythm. Jeremy and Melissa found themselves outside, clinging to each other and kissing passionately, before he led her to his apartment, directing her along messy streets to his minimal abode. There upon the bed, naked and together, they made love. As he ran his hands over her skin and nuzzled and caressed her, she feverishly imagined him without a head, just his body between her legs, his torso upon her. And when she bit her lip with fervour, she saw herself, herself alone, as a child, with only a mask for a face, across a willing soul. Jeremy lavished her with care and attention, building each moment to an exquisite finish, before beginning again. A giving lover, in the hope of sensual return, he pleasured her before pleasing himself, at once, both under the influence and watching from afar, like the lead role in a porno flick. Detached. She gasped and moaned as he tickled her pubis with his steely protrusion, gripping her tight as he floated to an end, emitting a grunt of insular pleasure as he came forth.

Afterwards, they shared a cigarette and talked for a bit. Soon, she rolled over, content for his hirsute body to lay against her, but just as eager to fall asleep. Stoned and quite happy, Jeremy sat there for a while, listening to his breathing and the absing of the ambient break, the rise and fall of the techno revolt.

> *"Evening would fall, the sky would become all soft and mellow, the neighbours talking with Yvars would suddenly lower their voices"*
> Albert Camus
> *The Silent Men*

## 1

Unnaturally, the car broke down. It slowed to a crawl until it stalled completely and left the occupants stranded in the countryside, twelve miles west of Oranmore. The Capri, a stoney relic from the seventies, simply had enough and gave up the ghost upon the two-lane dirt track masquerading as a road. The owner and driver sat at the wheel in a befuddled, baffled silence, disappointed and saddened by the motors sudden demise. She twisted the key sharply in the ignition, crunching the pistons and plugs, each attempt to start the car, growing steadily in aggression and futility. Beside her, Melissa wrapped her hair around her finger, awaiting the breakthrough that would send life spluttering from the walnut dashboard to the long-neglected engine, but each crank of the shaft only sounded worse as the revs hollowed and died.

"We're stuck," she said, finally defeated by the

obstinate speedster, that was content to idle on the track in a coolly, grey languor. The three women, traveling refugees from the communist enclave, pondered what to do.

Jemima, the beast's owner, was in a defiant mood, insisting that she stay with the car, hoping against hope for its regeneration. Melissa suggested calling a tow-truck, no way was she walking twelve miles. A discussion ensued before they settled on the pick-up truck, the third passenger calling from her mobile phone, over-coming the poor reception in the hilly countryside, connecting on the third attempt, through the AA, to a local breakdown service. Scores of trippers often made the desolate run to the scary isolation of the Atlantic cliff-top, driving or trekking along hidden roads, led only by the natural light of the twinkling stars or the booming sun, but the scenery was less postcard pictur-esque, than abnormally barren. The scape was poverty-stricken and desolate, its verges decked with crabby foliage and the thin brown husk of peat bogs. And as you pounded down the tracks, occasionally you could glimpse the far distant vision of a lone wanderer, trudg-ing through fields, gallantly protecting the interests of his animals.

"How long for the truck?" asked Jemima.

"At least an hour."

"So we'll just have to stew here," she said in disgust.

The three of them pushed the car to a grassy verge, shoved the two wheels up, onto a muddy bank and set-tled down to wait.

"Maybe not such a good idea," mumbled Lieza, the

one with the mobile phone. Jemima shot her a look through austere blue eyes. "Well I'm sorry ok. I thought the trip might alleviate the pressure of the party. I wasn't to know. And besides, I did not force you to come."

"It's this clap-trap hunk of a machine. Don't you ever have it looked at?"

"Often! I often send it for a service."

"Oh oh. To some brazen mechanic, who only puts his head under the bonnet, gives it the all-clear and then charges a fortune. An extortionate hooker, I'll bet."

"This has never happened before. It's always been so loyal."

"Loyal!? It's a machine. It has no commitment to you. Its not the party and you are not the party and you are not the party leader. You do not understand its machinations, its limitations and its sheer bullheaded-ness. And yet, you treat it as an object of love. Garner it with more care and attention than any man will give any woman and when it fails to work, you wonder why!" Lieza shook her head as her thoughts jumbled. "Oh, I don't know. Maybe we party people aren't meant for the countryside."

The communist social was built from the split of the socialist action group, a legitimate though once minor party on campus at the university of Oranmore. Now a major player in policy decision, it was littered with influential drunks and oafs and increasingly given to conservative lurches. Its administration, censorious and bullying was the emerging ruling class of the student body, constantly indulging in nauseous frat-boy behaviour and back-breaking stunts. The communist social, its off shoot, splinter group was a piece of feminie resistance, its members, at one together, refusing to kneel for the taciturn authoritarians. Yet its organisation was ramshackle. The arranged commune was little more than a series of dilapidated squats and bunks and it had a tiny political influence. It was easily mocked.

"Not for the city, not for the countryside. What are we party people built for?"

Above the three, a noisy squall of gulls flew fresh from the ocean, in a formation V.

"Perhaps we're not built for the party," said Melissa.

"And if we leave the party what then? With whom shall we belong? The apes of the Action group?"

Jemima looked across with a frown. "This is a solidarity or it is nothing. These years sacrifice will not be wasted. And the party allows a stiffening... back. A perfect education for perfect means."

She looked stern. Of the three, Jemima was the most stringent member, displaying steely resolve in defence of the party.

"I believe in it as much as you," cut in Melissa. "But when we qualify, we achieve our results and we walk to the job interviews and we come face to face with an action man, what then? Can you see them offer us the post? Their secret society is everywhere now. And if we get a job? Always passed over for promotion, always overlooked because of our communist links! I mean, will it always be a falcon around our necks?"

"It may take time," interrupted Lieza. "But we

shall infiltrate their companies. At least we are learning industry."

"Is it just a friendship thing?" asked Melissa, as a loaded and precarious process of thought came to a heavy end. "You know, is it just so that we can label ourselves, to be able to identify with the others? Are we to become uniformed students, all tagged indifferently and treated... badly, just so that we can affiliate ourselves? Assume an already held position, but with a discredited company?"

"We have our principles," protested Jemima. "We accept them as good."

"Oh the words of men in the mouth of babes."

"You're a good example," said Melissa to Lieza. "Is it only for the ease, that you're a party member?"

"Partly but I am a dedicated supporter."

"Perhaps. But that is me also. Wholeheartedly, I offer my support, but to what? No. Very little I see does the party stand for me."

To be sure, the party had long ago fallen into disrepute, but the flipside of communism is an interesting one. Whether in substance or stature or name alone, the route from dialectical communism, invariably leads to anarchism. And once an anarchist, the path returns is simple.

"Let's sit in the car and wait, shall we?"

The three clambered inside, sheltering from the early winters rain. Jemima gunned the ignition once again, again to no avail. In the shell of the Capri and with the sonorous radiowaves as dead as the battery, all the women could do was wait for the pick-up truck.

## 2

It arrived with a tootle, the mustachioed man at the wheel, clenching and unclenching his sternocleid neck muscles, at the sight of three stranded girls. He stuck his head under the hood and then attached jump leads between the two engines. Within five minutes, the Capri was purring over, Jemima, absolutely delighted with the motor's progress. Indelicately, she drove it off the verge and made an about-turn toward Oranmore. Under the blare of the radio noise, the girls were peculiarly quiet. Melissa wondered about her future with the party and her future without. Already in their second university year, the climate of the age called for affiliation. An unrecognised, insidious class system had steadily built up in the free state republic. An anonymous hierarchy taking up positions on an unseen board. Progress through the ranks was a powerplay, consisting of networking, influence and family affairs. An adherence to the dictates of the social doctrine was not a recognised qualification. The class ridden hedonism of the socialist students, the cider and champagne swillies was the standard, accepted behavioural pattern, that unlocked key doors for the impressionable and willing Action men body. In fact, the honorary chairperson of the socialist cavalcade was none other than J.M Guyae, chairman elect of the bank of the free state. And it was he, along with the banks governors, that played the tune to which this nations confused and gentle politicians would ultimately bark. In a vicious circle of ever increasing proportions, to be outside the archaic system was to be outside the sphere of influence. Lieza would walk away if a better alternative appeared, Jemima was a firm believer, but Melissa was viewing the party with a new antagonism.

"We must do this again sometime," Lieza muttered darkly as the boxy, warehouse city of Oranmore came glistening over the horizon. It was turning into a wet and miserable evening and the analytical drudgery of the day's disappointments was looming.

"Can I trouble you for petrol money?" asked Jemima, as she stopped at no. 27.

"You're crazy, aren't you?" said Lieza in disbelief. Melissa passed across some change and the two passengers got out and entered the renovated squat. It was tie-dye style, a mixed bag of acidy colours and swirling distractions, lovingly crafted in a cheap and cheerful fashion, by the occupants and party members. In a haze of reflected light, it was comforting in its familiarity.

"I met a new man," said Melissa to Lieza as they settled down. "I'm seeing him again."

Lieza looked up in surprise. "Oh really!" She sounded a little upset, her short phrase caught in the throat. "And is he the one casting aspersions upon the sisterhood?"

"He is influential. But you knew this could never

last. The flow is just too restricted."

"Yes. But for now, what do you suggest? Leaving the university?" asked Lieza.

"It's a possibility, yes."

Lieza looked incredulous. "What! And fend out there? It may not be the garden of Eden, but it's good here!" Melissa was flustered and defensive. Lieza continued: "It would be foolish to finish now. For all its faults, the university offers a few guarantees and could save you from a career in insurance."

"I don't know," Melissa said. "It's early days yet, I suppose."

"And who is the new man, come to sweep you off your feet?"

"His name is Jeremy."

# 3

Andrews goose stepped to attention. Arup was summoning him through speakerphone. He stood for presentation, gritting his teeth as Arup, slouched in a chair, engulfed himself with the effulgence of his own slow-breaking wind. Andrews retched and attempted to rise above it, rocking on his heels. Under his nostrils, air wafted.

The reconstruction was complete on the top floor. The seventh level had been converted entirely into Arup's office. He beckoned Andrews further inside who consciously strolled to the window frame and opened a sash. It was one of the bizarre anomalies of this city... that the foundation had only multie-story car parks for competition. Perhaps in unconscious homage the city was preparing for aquamarine devastation, its crazy planning the baseline for the factory style continuation of inward structural collapse. Any trace of vertigo was purely psychological.

Behind black glasses, Andrews felt the cooling breeze, sniffing in its essence. Refreshed, he turned to face Arup, the growing stone at the centre. Since the refurbishment, Arup had become increasingly withdrawn. The new office had welcomed him with its lofty grandeur and entranced him with its mahogany resolve. In here, Arup, the expanding businessman would blossom. He pictured visions of EU superstates, global clocks and kept the board table to himself. For his canvas! For Arup, at the height of his powers and replete with a burgeoning, birthing mind had become an artist. Protection in place and delegatory duties a pleasant aside. Arup was free to paint his intergalactic conceptions with which to woo an adoring public; from the sheltered darkness of his seventh level office.

"The view is good for artistry, no?" said Andrews to the non-plussed Arup.

"Inspirational!"

"Things are going well," continued Andrews. "Profit is up 20% and the climate is more stable."

Inside the club, Arup had planted his own dealers and rigourized the door search. Confiscations were a gratis bonus and everyone flocked for the good pills. Kicking and screaming this town was being dragged on. The drum had spun and the people followed the leader. And ironized by success, Ove Arup had ideas in mind. Ideas that reached to the growling pit of his bloated stomach.

"I think we should change the Netherlands flight path," continued Andrews. "Or alternate for a time."

"Umm, you're right," grumbled Arup. "Hook him up with someone in London. Whaddya say? Send the boy home?"

"Okay. That shouldn't be a problem."

"Good. Go. And get me some pizza."

Andrews departed and left Arup to his reveries.

# 4

On flight 404, Jeremy buried his head in a book awaiting the hostess and his complimentary drink. "Cocacola, please" he said as she followed the trolley along the aisle. Satisfactorily, the pilot took the plane in, taxiing the airbus to safety and parking up in a London airport sideway. S ambled lively, through arrivals happy to be among strangers and onrushing crowds. In the traditional manner, he caught the Piccadilly line to London central and hopped off at the north end.

He had instructions to meet a contact at 14.30. There merchandise would be inspected, arrangements came to and agreements made. But that wasn't for another four hours.

In a glacial café, filled with icy artifacts, the behooded Jeremy took a table and ordered a coffee. There he sat, sipping his coffee, smoking cigarettes and watching the TV set, that was propped upon a marble green pillar; it was an odd juxtaposition in the silvery interior. Only the news could add the required respectability to the surround and inevitably, Jeremy surrendered once again to its hypnotic message. He watched past the quakes and the nuclear winter, the gravelly newsreader sturdy under fire. He introduced shots of the EU army, peacekeeping on the Balkans borders, galvinising their strength against the scourge of Kalarosvan terrorism. Interviewing a major, the soldier showed the utmost composure in a pressurised situation, the camera no threat after blasts of gunfire. They were there to protect the refugees, still resident in the fields and tents; to distribute food and essentials, so that they, the political refugees, may at least subsist away from their homes and jobs. At that moment their houses were tumbling, their roofs aflame with ignorance and brutality; bombs were dropping on strategic targets, civil unrest was rife and a Kalarosvan mutiny was forecast.

"We're here for their own good," said the major under composure. The news moved on. The unofficial spokesman appeared.

"We've 'ad a breakthrough."

For sure, whatever it was, was lost under a stream of double talk and Gallic slang. Jeremy drew a blank as the screen played on. He finished his coffee and ordered another. The pretty waitress dropped it to his table in the unfluttered bistro.

"I apologize," she said. "It's quiet in here." She spun around the elegantly empty café. "But not too quiet for you, no?"

"No," said Jeremy. "Not at all, it's very calming."

"Oh good. Normally we are busier, but today... I don't know." She was attractive in her indecision and her gilded accent.

"Where are you from?"

She was Eastern European and a working student. "If you're not busy," said Jeremy, "would you like to join me for a coffee? I only have a little bit longer to wait and then..."

"...and then you're gone." She laughed. Jeremy smiled in reply. He bought a cappuccino and heard about her life. Before he left he took her number.

"I'm only here for a couple of days. If you like, we could meet up tonight?"

"That would be nice" she said. If he called her at seven, they would meet later that night.

"Okay," said Jeremy and went to his appointment.

# 5

At 19.00, Jeremy rang Maria, the waitress. They arranged to meet in Space, an East end nightclub, specialising in eighties electronica. He waited by the bar posing in sweet lassitude, until he spotted her. Brushing back her fair hair, she came over to him.

"I must confess," she said in a lilting European accent, "that I am very excited about tonight." Touchingly, she ran her finger along his clothes and nuzzled his ears as they stood at the counter. Jeremy willingly fell to her sweet embrace. He talked seductively and serenely to her, he listened to her words and eventually led her to a quiet corner, where their fires were stoked and blue neon shrouded them. Burning with desire, at 04.00 Maria took Jeremy outside and she langoured in a doorway while he laconically seduced her. They continued in a taxi, playing games with the driver until they paid their fare and duly entered her apartment.

Inside, their ardour levelled. For a moment or two the picture was shaky while she nervously handed him a glass of wine as he threw his jacket on the couch. Taking the wine, he took a reassuring gulp, coolly placed the glass upon the counter and passionately kissed her.

Leading him by the hand, she led him to her bedroom where she took him on the bed. With wrapped around legs, they tore off their tops. Jeremy undoing her bra, before superbly pulling off his t-shirt to reveal his feathery torso. As he went down again, she pushed him away, up, off her body. Half-naked, with hands squarely on his chest, she pushed him to a wicker seat. Compliant, he sat slant-eyed in the bedroom light, watching her as she undressed. For him, she stood naked, refusing to let him touch her, but eager for his look.

So, on he looked, as she began a hypnotic dance, perfectly timed to reveal herself, piece by piece. She showed herself crouched down, demonstrated her bending over, occasionally moaning to herself, when she looked at Jeremy between moving from pose to pose. In the seat, Jeremy was heated and icy. His body singed with the thrill, apparent in his calculated hand motion and long, heavy breaths. Still clad in jeans, he dropped his left hand on his crotch and stroked his chin with the other. Maria moved from pose to pose and S put his hand to his breastbone, rolling palm along downy fluff and absently tweaking his nipples.

He reached out to her again and she gently pushed away his arm and continued her erotic design of a one-woman ballet. Settling back and with his prick erect under the denim, Jeremy watched her ass as she paced for him, softly gliding along the rug.

"You tell me what to do," she said.

After a dignified pause, S told her to lie on the bed and open her legs. With lips like roses, he directed her into a series of positions and manifestations. Coldly, he calculatedly formulized the poses, with such precision, that she could stand it no more and begged for him to take her.

# 6

So, no more heroes. Just a species of blank-faced astronauts who bear their cross without burden. Individually, Jeremy bore no remorse, being only a willing accomplice to the existential waitressing. Absurdity has been assimilated, consciously or not and any sense of ease is purely personal. The pretty, blonde Eastern European was doing little more than playing the starring role and all her actions appeased the baying packs of devils that lurked in wait for that one moment of defensiveless collapse, in which would come forth the cat, the witch, the bat and the newt. And so, Jeremy, mentally resolved, left at seven the next morning, sauntering out into the open air, leaving Maria to a deep and dreamy sleep.

Guilty problem fixed and with business to come, he returned to his B+B, to skin an early joint and wait for time to come around. Yesterday had been unproductive. Bruce Di'anno, the contact supplier had been cagey and paranoically intense. Clearly, when introduced to S, Di'anno was precariously fraught. He was jittery and twitchy and flapping his body to an unheard epic rhythm. Both immediately distrustful, they arranged another meet for today. Jeremy had phoned Andrews to tell him he was wary and was instructed to continue, but without commitment. To delve into the pit, yet be prepared to run at a moments notice.

Di'anno was indeed tense and uptight. Progressively and systematically his side-holding business was being torn away. The hard work and effort he had invested over the years was being undermined by a sharper, less sociable breed of mercenaries. Ten years ago, he and Arup had been untouchable distributive-moguls in a booming industry, laundering cash, women, drugs and real estate. They lived a high-cut life, always well-turned out, an intrinsic cog in the secular machine of the underground power elite. Nearing the zenith of their glory days, the fat, controlling Arup, realizing they were overstepping the pinnacle of accepted metropolitan excess, had fled. Di'anno, addicted to the style, remained, over-confident and under-cautious. Now, his thin stream of economy was ebbing, the respite of the receding flow only allowing him to further wallow in sentimentality and fuel his dependency. With every new face and every new job, he got caught in the glare of unforgiving lights, others intolerant of his own inward, sympathetic bleating.

And so, for Bruce at least, any deal or transaction was a blustering mess of tension and knots and fluttering spots of pressurised excitement when he felt his heart about to explode into space. A lunar blood-line of madness run from his nostrils to the base of his spine, imbuing any situation in a raging battle between self and ego, manifest in a jumbled stream of consciousness with which he assailed his audience.

Bells were ringing when Jeremy arrived in the seedy

West end office. Arup's idea of a two-strung arrangement was rapidly disappearing. Jeremy, under his own volition, was preparing to veto the deal at any moment. Di'anno was maniacal, nearing a fall and his business nearly at an end. He had been dead on his feet when Andrews had called and to himself, he was adamant that this was the crank-up call he needed. Across the table and with emotive hands, he spelled out to his client, his plan of action. The medicine bottles were in a suburban town. They would drive there today, avoid being followed and he would display the pills for Jeremy's discretionary eye. For Di'anno, it couldn't be simpler. However he had neglected to inform Andrews the difficulties of his financial position and had to operate through other streams. But he was wading through others' pollution. As a player he was finished and everyone knew it, but his big-time questioning and probes had alerted a ruthless and unscrupulous competition. Arup, for all his belly aches, was playing it large.

# 7

Spinning the wheel, Di'anno took the car off the slush-lined kerb. The two men lurched into the air as the tyres slumped onto the tarmacadam of the narrow, busy street. Di'anno gunned the engine, revving the motor in a show of crowd control, pedestrians hopping onto the sidewalk as the car cruised along the tight, yellow lines. Slowly and deliberately, Di'anno instinctively maneouvered through the jangly, bohemian avenues, indicating left, turning right and smoothly cornering onto the wider thorough-fares, the gold coast shopping palisades and into the heavy traffic. Oceans of people swaggered past, while the car idled in an everyday jam. Stopping and starting in conjunction with the myriad of lights, Di'anno skipped lanes, firstly, pulling up behind gas-guzzling lorries and vans – the undisputed kings of the roads – and attempting every possible escape towards a faster route, while Jeremy watched through the wind-shield, as the traffic gradually thinned and sped. Secondly, Di'anno, began losing composure as the flow reasonably steadied. He accelerated quickly, tailgating incessantly – zooming up to the bumper of the motor in front – before forcing the other driver over, or else, nipping to the side and violently passing them out. He would lurch forward at a tremendous rate, flooring the pedal with linear determinism, until he spotted a speed camera and broke sharply and suddenly, to avoid its flash. Di'anno blinked rapidly as he drove and continually flicked his head from side to side.

Taking the piss, thought S.

Jeremy could tolerate the erratic driving and the frisson it produced, but Di'anno's incessant yapping was irritating and an overt distraction. As the car tallied forth, Jeremy had to resist the urge to punch him in the face and shove him out the door. Di'anno, permanently strung on cocaine and amphetamines, displayed an inability to grit his teeth and progress. All his talk and words were a low-cut montage of gibberish and alien speak, a nonsensical exercise in indulgence, being as he was unable to keep his mouth shut. He squinted through his lids and peppered his lone conversation with a string of cuss words.

In mid-curse, he swung off the secondary road onto the six-lane M7. Now, in evenflow, Jeremy gripped the suit-hangar, stuck to the roof, in steady eyed silence and Di'anno flung the motor into the third lane and glued the pedal to the felted carpet mat. Intermittently, he talked self-pitying garbage as S peered out, calmly, at the twilit autoway. Obviously making good time, they took the junction to the borderline county, negotiating twisty, country streets until they arrived at a leafy shire hall. Behind them a Vauxhall Astra parked up in the bushes.

They announced themselves through the gate's intercom, the big, black blockade opening slowly for them, and they drove up the driveway. At the entrance, they were frisked by two well-dressed goons, who allowed them in and directed them where to go. The hall reeked with the fresh smell of new cash, immaculately designed with retro fashion and feng-shui positioning, and the walls were reverberating with disco. Somebody waved them into a room.

"Monsieur Cimino will see you soon. Wait here."

"This is studio 55 – more, more, more... more stories than ever, have I heard of this place. It's famous, an institution," said Di'anno to Jeremy.

It was malenky disappointment that if what he said was true, then he'd have to experience it with such company. Di'anno moved effortlessly from self-pitying schtich to sycophantic slobberings in a split-second, bouncing with glee as he poked and prodded items and pieces. "This is studio 55. You never heard of this?"

"No can't say I have."

"More powerful than the president."

Monsieur Cimino was a Canadian refugee, elderly in retrospect, yet the vibrant heart-throb behind the on going ecstasy revolt. A one-time activist in the sixties heyday, he had posed as Che Guevara in the swinging circles, wined and dined with Castro and took afternoon tea with Bob Marley. A curious anomaly, he was interested in the pure essence and disguised himself under the moloko of historical haze. Now, although past his physical prime, he was still an imposing presence in these hallowed walls of his factory and home. For, Monsieur Comino was none other than Mister Hitachi, the reclusive genius behind the emergence of MDMA –

uncut, producing it in a home-made boiling pot and distributing throughout the nation. Di'anno had bluffed his way in, relying on trust and abusing good will.

Cimino strolled in and took his applause with customary cool. He gestured for the two to sit. "Mister Cimino," sucked Di'anno, "it's good to see you. How are you keeping? I was just saying to my colleague here, it's a fucking excellent place you've got." Wearing a strained, desperate look on his face, Bruce attempted to shake his hand, clinging far too long, pumping too hard before making clumsy attempts to bond through the power of touch. Two protection agents stood up, Di'anno stood back.

"Okay," said Cimino, "down to business. I have a heated turntable awaiting me."

"Oh, you make music?" leered Di'anno. Jeremy came to the rescue. "Hey man, we gotta get back soon."

"Rushing back so quickly," gurgled Cimino, stifling a chuckle. "You're right, too. Anyway, let's see what we have." An agent produced two large containers and opened them on the table.

"Your order, gentlemen."

Bruce bent forward. "This is excellent, so fucking excellent." He let out a breath of anticipated shock and then began fumbling. "But Mister Cimino, sir... I... we have a slight problem. Two goddamn cocksucking debtors of mine didn't deliver. I... that is... we... ah, we don't have..."

"...the money?"

"We don't have all the money... but... but I can assure you... We will. My colleague and I are only a day away from collecting."

Jeremy listened under a veneer of impotent frustration, but gracefully and with a clockwork benevolency, Cimino accepted what they had and gave them half the deal, more than the notes were worth. Di'anno thanked him profusely and Jeremy bid him good day. As they drove off, a celestial rainbow could be seen, curving from one end of the sky to the other. Yet the night grew darker and when, with a quick backward glance, Jeremy looked over his shoulder, he saw the looming headlights of the Vauxhall Astra.

8

"Did you see that?"

"What?"

"That." Jeremy gestured to the rearview. Di'anno looked back. "What!? That car? What about it?"

"It pulled out at the same time as us. It was parked up in the bushes."

"Yeah?! Ah man, don't worry about it. Just some yokel." Di'anno, boosted by the lift of the deal was boisterous and cocky. He tunelessly drummed the steering-wheel and sporadically pointed his index finger at Jeremy while going 'doo-whop'. Small drops of runny snot were being wiped up the fascistic undergrowth on his upper lip. It was right about then that Jeremy had the urge to kill him.

"I'm telling you, that car is following us."

"Hey look, relax man. Just some shepherd with nowhere else to go. Don't worry about it. We'll soon be out of the dark and back into the bright lights of the big city." He punched him jocularly on the knee. "Tell you what, what say, we go celebrate, if you know what I mean. Bribe a few ladies with the good stuff. Yeah, yeah. The ones without any charm, heh, heh, heh."

"The hell with that. Pull the car over. Let this fool

pass us out."

"Ok, ok. Whatever you want."

"See, look," he said as the Datsun took a hedgerow and the Astra drove on by. "Nothing to worry about. Nada, not a thing."

One hundred metres along the narrow road the Astra was parked up.

"Oh shit!"

As their paths crossed in reverse, Jeremy looked asunder, into the eyes of two faceless killers.

"Oh shit!" repeated Di'anno.

Suddenly accelerating, the Datsun roared upon its way. The Astra likewise, followed in pursuit, its driver gunning it for all it's worth, its front bumper catching the rear of the other, slowing it down, both cars skidding a little. The room for maneouver was slim, the screeching wheels pebble-dashing the straggly fauna, the Astra swinging slightly into the foliage.

The Vauxhall eased a bit, its speedometer dropping as the driver regained control. Di'anno in the Datsun pushed it harder. The gap lengthened, only yards but it was enough. Taking twisty turns and tight bends, he kept his lead, once or twice, veering up in the darkness of the sidings. Struggling to keep the wheel, Di'anno pressed even further, hitting a straight stretch of road, the engine booming with excess and the tyres squealing with immutable speed. Behind them, the Astra, a better machine, came rushing forth, the gap, now nothing at all.

From ayonder came the beaming lights of a third vehicle, about to swing into their path. The Datsun revved and screeched, shot past the lights of the oncoming tractor chugging along, right into the face of the Astra. Realising it wasn't going to stop, the flat-capped farmer, tried to steer his hunk of junk away, but got caught in the crossfire of the two screeching cars, it lost its momentum, tottered on two wheels and eventually toppled over, the driver scrambling for safety out the other side. On, the two cars raced, Di'anno and the Datsun searing the macadam and at the wheel, Bruce himself, chattering with fear and whistling through rotting teeth and bloody gums. Beside him, Jeremy sat, stern with adrenaline. In a moment of unforgiving glory, they hit the autoway, the orange motor rising off the ground as it slammed onto the tar. Skidding into flow, two automobiles, coming up behind, careered crazily along the white lines, sending flying a cloud of brake dust and smoke, the Astra steaming through the residue. In and out, the cars dodged, wildly, between the traffic, caught in crossbeams, and the overhanging rays of the night lights reflecting upon the steely roofs in a prism of yellowy hue.

Now, sweating at the brow, Bruce, obnoxious at the helm, sped past vehicles with only inches to spare, the two cars, dancing through the flow, seen from above like the choreographed moves of a metal and windshield musical, under road bridges and past service stations and stop 'n' shops. But still the Astra gained, until Di'anno, in a show of irregular thinking and with only a second to spare, swung the Datsun across the lanes and spun off the autoway into a junction. The Astra, going too fast, its faceless driver too slow to react, got caught in the second lane, blocked by a lorry to the left and had to continue on.

"Phew, how about that then?" said a gurning Di'anno, his eyes like pissholes in the snow above his finger stroking his moustache. Pursing his lips in contempt, Jeremy was stoney-eyed.

"Who the hell were they?"

"Jeez, I dunno... I dunno. The people against Cimino? Opportunistic thugs? I dunno, but boy was I good." Di'anno drove in smugness, repeatedly saying, "Wow, was I good. Was I good or what?" So good, in fact that he had to stop at a filling station to relieve himself. He took his car keys, but by the time he stepped back outside. Jeremy had stolen the car and all of the drugs.

# 9

Arup listened through speakerphone.

"I'm mad as hell Arup. Mad as hell. You call me up, after all these years, those goddamn years and ask me a favour. I do you a favour, I look after your man. I go to huge trouble to help you out – and man, I'm clean now, been clean for years, since you ran out, you chicken bastard – I help you out. I put my life on the line. I take him to Cimino. I get him a good deal. I risk my life and my cock-sucking limb to get away and then your goddamn employee – your employee Arup. Don't forget he's *your* employee – your goddamn employee RIPS ME OFF! And now, I'm as mad as hell. Arup? Are you listening to me Arup? Answer me, you cocksucker!"

Arup pressed the mute button and motioned for Andrews to come over.

"Andrews, if that man ever rings again, have him shot."

"Okay."

# 10

The communists were on the streets. Jemima was marching from the front, holding a placard and leading the chant... 'No Bombs in the Balkans, No Bombs in the Balkans.' A group of Association members and unaffiliated layabouts had gathered to protest against the continued bombing campaign, pacing through Oranmore to rally the valued support of the people of the Free State. In the middle of the mass, Melissa and Jeremy walked side by side, an anonymous centrepoint to the shouting hordes. They marched from one end of the town to the other, unhindered by the uniformed police but undoubtedly under the surveillance of their covert branch and thus, five minutes later, Jeremy and Melissa found themselves squeezed together in a cosy little bar, unwilling to get intertwined with the public speakers and their valid, but uninformed rhetoric.

"I missed you," she said.

He wrapped his arm around her and held her close. He'd arrived home two days before, the car left on a bridge, somewhere in Wales, and delivered the pills to Andrews at the Third Eye Foundation. Handsomely paid, he'd boozed and schmoozed the night away, contacting Melissa the following day.

"The party," he said "is it very political?"

"No, not very. But we do have principles to uphold. And we exercise our rights."

"Aha."

She looked up a little sadly. Leaning forward, she took a careful sip of her drink before continuing...

"We mainly do it for companionship, you know. Warmth and affection."

He nodded. "Right," he said slowly.

"Is it different for a man? No ties, no binds, free to do as you please?" She settled back into the seat, turning her body towards him. He smiled playfully at her beauty.

"Solitary or solidary...? Yeah I suppose it is, but there are a lot of...shall we say... 'confused' ... young men about. Disturbed homosexuals, blotting the natural course of evolution and too much infatuated with their fathers. In fact, any male who inserts an object into his anus for pleasure is mentally ill and shouldn't be allowed near our children."

"I'd leave the party in a second, like that," she said, clicking her fingers, "if I could find the warmth elsewhere. You never know, could even fall in love."

"You never know," said Jeremy, off the cuff and staring straight ahead. Melissa smiled wanly and shutting her watery eyes, kissed him on the cheek.

I suppose, she thought, with a little time and courage... but she decided not to hand in her party membership, just yet.

# 11

They spent the night together. Melissa silently wondering about the scratches on his back. Tonight, Jeremy was particularly useless. A little drunk and too stoned to function properly, it was a sweaty anticlimax, coming too soon and bowling out early. His pathetic performance left her hardened and ever so frustrated. Lovingly consoling him, she accepted his sniffling apologies and listened to his pitiful excuses.

"I'm sorry, I've had a hectic week." He told her of his London sojourn, the theft of the car from outside the filling station.

"So you just left him stranded?"

"Yeah and took his drugs too!"

It was about this time that Jeremy caught up with himself. Self-satisfied, his body at rest, like any real man, he entered that domain of blissful indifference – the elevated superman, pleased with his accomplishments of the night and the week. It's in this domain, that the myth of the female orgasm is not entertained and man is the ultimate beast – the hunter, warrior, planning for his future, his body centrifugal, like the nucleus of the atom and everything and everybody else, merely the protons that revolve around the centre. Pea soup exoticism, the pure poetry of the masculine mind.

"Pardon?"

"Today? What are you doing today? Later on?"

"I have an essay to finish. We're coming to a modular ending." She lay on her back and stretched out on the bed, pulling away from Jeremy. "I suppose I should get some sleep," she said and turned over and shut her eyes. As she turned away, Jeremy was shot through with feelings of guilt and lay down next to her, burying his head in her hair and placing his arm around her.

# 12

Melissa actually slipped off early the next morning, leaving Jeremy a note by his stash of marijuana. Waking up at approximately 11.00, he was surprised to see she had gone and blithefully stumbled to the television set, switching it on and flopping onto his couch. He went to roll a joint – a good way to start any day, especially those who don't buy into the perversity that is breakfast cereal – and saw the note. 'Had to go. Call me tonite,' he read and then put it aside. It was moments like these that the anarchist creed paid off. Free of the number-crunching and relaxing in the understated, one-sided glory of the night before, the morning after. Jeremy had nothing to do except pass judgement on the daytime TV, blissfully stoned and fighting for the rights of the humble housewife, whose senses are continually assaulted by reams of patronizing drivel – like this. The housewife's favourite, that's me, thought Jeremy, as he damned yet another presenter.

Bumbled into action by sheer boredom after a while, he showered and dressed and made his way toward the city-town. In his stoned state, the utter mess the councilmen had made of this town-city, was twice as confounding. Supposedly, a major player in the free state economy and the west coast capital, Oranmore somehow revelled under the title of city, but its selection, its planning and its sheer bloody size could grace it only with a towns amenities. The bent council say they give the people what they need, but invariably, when it all falls apart, the people are told that they got what they wanted. Its shambolic streets, its mess of vehicles and the Celtic ingenuity behind traffic-lit roundabouts, could only indicate town in backward flux, lost and in strife.

And for the ambling stoner, the locals piercing, penetrating and rather impolite and jealous stares only added hostilities to what should be a pleasant wander. And thus, Jeremy strolled along the main streets trying to avoid the gaze of the dim-witted youths and writers, who believe the fashion of the day is the retarded chic of tongue in lower lip and dribble down the corners of their mouths, while peering out with soulless eyes. The Bronx, he had heard one boy call it, just prior to stabbing another. Everybody has to pay their dues.

Jeremy knocked on Gondys door and was welcomed warmly by his fellow fugee.

"Ah, the traveler returns. How goes it?"

"Good, thank you," said S.

They settled down for more televisual delights and Jeremy spilled the beans about his weeks escapades. About Maria the waitress and his relationship with Melissa. He told his stories matter-of-factly, but they still hung heavy in his heart. Talking about it eased the burden.

"You jammy bugger," said Marcus.

On the TV, 24 hours Sky News was screening an interview with the Governor of the EU, the president of the British Isles, from a tent somewhere along the Montenegron border. The volume was down, the sounds were up and the camera was fixed upon his head, on his thinning thatch and his earnest skeletal face.

"Come on, your sultry adventures have given me a thirst."

The two ventured outside, into the nuclear winter and under a vibrant sky, clear with frost and freezing cold, they entered the Realm, settled at a table and chatted a while. The obligatory TV was on, Sky news playing, the headlines repeating and the interview beginning again.

"We're here to help," said the Governor of the EU, the president of the British Isles. The piece moved on, outside the tent, into the fields, to the pictures of thousands of political refugees and the beloved leader of the EU and British Isles walking amongst them. Through a cleared path, they pushed the people back, who cheered as the saviour appeared, arms outstretched in the design of the cross.

It's just like Camus said – a man only crucifies himself these days to be seen from a further distance.

*"I am going to tell the story of an alien.*
*The story I am going to tell..."*
Albert Camus
*The First Man*

# 1

In Mikhail Bulgakov's *The Master and Margarita*, there is a chapter – no. 13 – entitled 'Enter the Hero'. In this chapter Ivan Bezdomny, a Russian poet has been ensconsed in a mental hospital by Dr. Stravinsky after a day of bizarre events that include a death, a talking cat, a magician and Pontius Pilate. In his room, on his bed, a mysterious stranger visits Bezdomny. Bezdomny tells the visitor of his story, while in other rooms, patients are being admitted. In room 119, a fat man with a purple face keeps shouting "encore, encore"; Bezdomny grows sad as he tells the story of the death of his friend and how the magician was in fact Satan. The visitor knows him, this devil called Woland, able to pass through time.

The visitor, having pinched a set of keys from an absent-minded nurse, is able to come and go across the balcony, through the window grilles, as he pleases, yet admits that he is destitute. He doesn't leave the hospital, because he has nowhere to go. In fact, he would have loved to have met Woland, for it is also because of

Pontius Pilate that he has been committed, because of a novel he wrote. When Bezdomny asks the writer his name, the visitor angrily replies that he is a master and of no name because he has renounced it.

The master goes on to tell of the money he had won in the lottery, enabling him to live a contained life, whilst finishing his novel. For breaks, he used to take walks and lunch in restaurants. One day, he sees a flower-seller, wearing a black dress and carrying yellow blooms. In a crowd of thousands, they see no-one but each other and the Master was struck, "less by her beauty, than by the extraordinary loneliness in her eyes." Side by side and in perfect silence, they walked along a street, until she asked if he liked her flowers. No, he says and promptly falls in love. Embarrassed, she throws the flowers away and guiltily he picks them up again. She won't take them and he carries them until she throws them away again and takes his hand. Afterwards, "love leaped up, out at us like a murderer jumping out of a dark alley. It shocked us both." They had loved each other for years without knowing it and had merely been living with other people. The Master, for his part cannot remember the name of the girl he was living with. The girl with the flowers says that she came out for him to find her and if it hadn't happened, she would "Have committed suicide because her life was Empty." Having fallen in love on the embankment below the Kremlin wall, they talked like they'd known each other all their lives and arrange to meet again and "soon that woman" became the Masters "mistress". She'd visit him every day and everyday he would wait for her, his heart beating faster at every sound. The strain of waiting would give him hallucinations, seeing things on the table. They tell no-one of their affair, not her husband, nor his friends. At this point, the Master refuses to reveal his name. So utterly in love, the couple were inseperable and believed fate had brought them together and they were together for eternity. Thus, in the heat of the summer, the Master worked feverishly on his novel and the book entranced the woman so much, he was almost jealous of it, reading it and rereading as she was.

The Master continues his story, but it gets more disjointed and confused to the very depths of their love, until they're hushed by the sounds of wheels in the corridor. In room 120, a new patient is admitted. A man who keeps asking for his head.

# 2

"Arr yo fallowing me?"

Jeremy faced his accuser. It was one of Arup's expelled henchboys. "No," said Jeremy and continued walking and window-shopping. But his accuser blocked his path.

"Yo wark 'n dat clubb down dere?"

"No."

"Ya do, ya do. I seen ya."

"I don't know what you're talking about. Now if you'll excuse me." His accuser didn't move, staring at him, his mouth agape with mindless aggogery. Jeremy moved on, stepping past him only to be blocked again. Putting his hand on his accusers shoulder, he gently shoved him aside and proceeded. Rearing up like a pig oinks, his accuser called after him...

"Warr goin ta ged ye. D'ya understand? Oo arr. Warr goin ta ged ya."

Befuddled, Jeremy looked back to see him wiping skin of his chin.

# 3

Overnight, from the fields along the Montenegron border, the refugees vanished. One day, thousands of the dispossessed huddled in amongst tents and flotsam and debris, herded from their homes to live like that. A saviour appeared and next day, gone, all gone, nothing but a rubbish-strewn field for memory. There were no mass graves, but the bombs were dropped.

In the Foundation, Jeremy encountered the other three. There was a groovy vibe, weaving from the walls as he stepped through the floor. "You fool," said an Italian. "Pull up a stool."

The DJ spun the discs for the night, filling the space with sounds and checked out the lights. The mirrorball, swinging through the blue and white strobes, the empty dancefloor shining.

"Arup's a happy man," said K.

"Hey, Nigel, Nige, don't give the dude a big head."

But the little dude up front didn't really know what he was doing. Jeremy stole the car on instinct, he hadn't given the cash to Di'anno and had left Arup's wad in a locker in Victoria bus station. Took it back with him of course. He was nothing if not honest. Arup and Andrews were evenly cool about the free haul, gave all four a little bonus that late December month.

"Good job man," said Nige. "Maybe you white boys not so stupid after all. Yes?"

Jeremy rolled a spliff on the counter. "What can I say, this boy got soul!"

"You missing all the trouble though. The peasants are revolting."

"Yeah, tell me about it. Some dumbfuck goon tried to smack me up outside. I showed him the hairs of my chinny chin chin." He licked the joint.

"Could you imagine them whispering in your ear at night," said an Italian.

"You drown first, yeah, ha ha," said the other. In the evolutionary scheme of things, this country must have been a test case. Maybe the first country in the world, where the gentler sex completely outclass the posturing proles. Centuries of priests and weird, twisted bishops have finally taken its toll.

Anyway, Proudhon and Tolstoy, the two Italians were building for attack. The mid-stream of this cyber-hell had slackened recently. The expelled henchboys had been peculiarly quiet of late, save for the occasional blatant threat, which had once been an everyday nuisance. In the interim, Arup had devised a third level of protection, allowing Tolstoy and Proudhon to fund a be-spoke army, answering to the Italians, but kept out of the management suite. Black-suited baldies now patrolled the Third Eye Foundation, adding a sheen of controlled menace and sophisticated sexuality. The country boys now ejected and banished from the Third Eye, were gathering outside, concocting vile plans of revenge and hissing at each other, as they tried feebly to devise a system of retribution. Sooner or later they were going to try and barge down the doors and overtake all stories of the club. They pictured themselves progressing through all levels until they reached the hallowed ground of the seventh-storey set-up, where Arup would be found, behind his desk ready for the guillotine.

Ove Arup was there now. Had been there for days. He no longer left the office. Ate, slept and worked from the top floor, spending his time splashing paint onto canvas, or otherwise, sitting, slumped in his swivel-chair, pulling at his straggly, reddening, lengthening beard and staring at his navel. He buzzed in his advocate, who appeared, as discreet as ever, to the finest point.

"Andrews," said Ove, looking up with the strangest, queerest look on his face and a mad glint in his eye. "Andrews," he said, "I think I'm pregnant."

"That so?" said Andrews, matter-of-factly.

# 4

It's easy to fall victim to the lure of the mighty dollar. Any upwardly-thinking businessman is easily duped by the idea of sleeping on a bed of hard cash, driven by dreams of excess, luxury and langour. Tonight the four of the Foundation were watching its all too predictable collapse. The scaffold of the structure of white-middle class America is weak, unsupported and easily exploited. Information, noise, advertisements and distractions are pumped continuously to an undiscerning mass, with neither the time, nor the inclination, to deconstruct and dissimulate the myriad of symbols, signs, pointers and markers. In fact, to be governed is to be watched over, inspected, spied on, directed, legislated, regimented, closed in, indoctrinated, preached at, controlled, assessed, evaluated, censored, commanded, all by creatures that have neither the right, nor wisdom nor virtue... To be governed means that at every move, operation or transaction one is noted, registered, entered in a census, taxed, stamped, priced, assessed, patented, licensed, authorized, recommended, admonished, prevented, reformed, set right, corrected. Government means to be subjected to tribute, trained, ransomed, exploited, monopolized, extorted, pressured, mystified, robbed; all in the name of public utility and the general good. Then, at the first sign of resistance or word of complaint, one is repressed, fined, despised, vexed, pursued, hustled, beaten-up, garroted, imprisoned, shot, machine-gunned, judged, sentenced, deported, sacrificed, sold, betrayed and to cap it all, ridiculed, mocked, outraged and dishonoured. That is Government and that is its justice and morality.

Meanwhile at some EU state summit or other, the president of the British Isles, Antony Hair, stepped down as Governor of the EU, only to be superceded by that corrupt faggot, Peter Mandelsohn. Personally... I blame the parents!!

*"In any case the figures of those old historians, like Procopious, weren't to be relied on; that was common knowledge. Seventy years ago, at Canton, forty thousand rats died of plague before the disease spread to the inhabitants. But, again, in the Canton epidemic there was no reliable way of counting up the rats. A very rough estimate was all that could be made, with, obviously, a wide margin for error. 'Let's see,' the doctor murmured to himself, 'supposing the length of a rat to be ten inches, forty thousand rats placed end to end would make a line of...'"*

Unkle Albert; Camus
*The Plague*

# 1

Marcus was leaving, booked himself a one-way ticket to the United States, destined for fame and fortune. Jeremy arrived to say goodbye, wish him the best and to smoke his skunk.

They skinned up together and Jeremy helped himself to the food. "Finally over?" he said.

"Yeah well!" sighed Marcus. "It has, in the words of Sartre... it has been an adventure." They lit the two joints and Jeremy pocketed a bottle of vodka.

"Very Zen."

They switched the telly on and Jeremy stole some books, you know, just taking back what was stolen from him.

The telly playing, the two stoned themselves to high heaven, sitting wide-eyed and amazed as the young Sir Ian Cullen flashed up. They watched on for hours, growing steadily higher, men smoking the time. Another out-of-body experience... floating in space for ever-more, until they returned and Marcus turned to Jeremy.

"What if..." said Marcus, "what if someone, some-where has discovered a mode of electrical transport, a travelling machine to skip from time to time, to travel the grid, from there to here to then, to biblical times across the world, wherever that may be. To our reincar-nated selves today, to the species of the future, to first the man and woman alone, second to the couple, from here to beyond and eternity, forevermore."

"What if..." hushed Jeremy. He pursed his lips. "Probably invented by a woman too," he said bitterly.

Marcus chuckled at the absurdity... and then left.

## 2

Wombles wobble... but they don't fall down.

# 3

"We have competition," began Andrews. "Things are gonna have to move quickly. Pete in the Netherlands has informed me of a rival firm, operating from the east. They're buying merchandise wholescale, and putting feelers on Jeeves. We've been undercut by 10% and there are rumours of rival foundations. This is large-scale pressure. They appear to be stalking us before busting our deals."

Arup frowned. "Do we know who they are?"

"We've had fleeting glimpses, but they're very good. I'm damned if I can find out their names."

"Are they a threat?"

"At this moment in time, no. But I fear with a little while, problems are going to develop."

Arup stood up and scratched his behind. He gently fondled his body, cradling his belly. These days isolation was wreaking havoc with the ventilation system. He hadn't slept in days, little bits of food hung on his beard and his feet stank.

"Right, I understand... malevolent forces closing on me. Even for all the debt mankind owes me, they still wish to torment and tease. Well, I'll squeeze them, squeeze them until they crack and fluids dribble out. Dry!"

Andrews nodded.

Arup rose up. "Call Peter. Find the times of any meets and arrangements they may have with Jeeves. Once you've done that, get Jeremy, and Nigel. I will not be made a fool of!"

Andrews saluted and departed.

Anxious, Arup walked in circles, pacing through his seventh-level office. Blood coursed from his mind to his flesh and bone, his head ticking over, ruminating on all the possible formulaes, combinations and permutations. He reached outlandish conclusions, came to impossible ends, all the while, the electricity and blood fusion, wiping him down with headaches and dumbness, until in a moment of dull collapse, he fell to the floor, paralysed by analysis, his thoughts black and a jumbled, white line of voices, flowing past his eye, triggering the key to the explosion in his stomach. He lay prone on the ground, incapacitated, rolling his eye, voyeuristically, to the rear of his head. He swelled and purged and then vomited up, over his own face and flecked his beard with spots of puke. 'I am reborn,' he thought.

Outside, in the secretarial suite, all in orange, Andrews was behind his desk, studying pictures of naked women, smiling for the camera, their cheeks wide open, licking the window.

# 4

Inversely, Melissa and Lieza were leaving university. Couldn't remember a thing from the last three months, the guiding eye of Professor G. William Domhoff, gone since summer and Professor Gus van Barnes, that ever elusive celtic impressionario, all lost at sea. Melissa phoned Jeremy as he was packing his bags for Holland and told him of her decision. Plans were formulating. Jeremy and Nigel K were tripping abroad, first of all, to seal a deal, secondly to size up the competition.

"When are you coming back?" she asked.

"Soon," he replied. "Just give me four days, before you go altogether."

"Okay."

Together, S and K, boarded an airplane, their destination, Interhuizen. There, they had to collect a bag of cash, purchase their wares and proceed further north, where they were to be met by Jeeves.

For Jeremy, it was an intriguing progression. The X amount of cash they were supposed to be collecting was becoming more and more attractive. Between himself and Nigel, to split the load in two was the thought playing in the back of his brain. Make a quick escape home and take off with Melissa.

They landed in Schipol airport, the sweet, succinct smell of grass, hitting them as they walked off the gang-plank.

"Will we go through with this?" asked Nigel.

"Don't see why not," said Jeremy. "But it's going to have to be fast. In and out, smash and grab and then a clean break."

They picked up a rent-a-car and drove smoothly over the pristine Dutch streets, out of the capital and into the tidy, irrigated countryside. A couple of hours later, they reached the picturesque town of Interhuizen. Stopping at a bank, they picked up a cash transfer and headed towards Jeeves. There the exchange was made, the gear loaded and the money placed in the safe inside a wall in Jeeves' studio. Shaking hands, Nigel inquired about any unwelcome visitors.

"No," lied Jeeves. "There's been no problems. We've had our usual, steady intake. Tell Arup he has nothing to worry about. Everything is hunky-dory, peachy-creamy, AOK."

Jeeves was an animated man and a blatant liar. There is nothing worse than a bad liar.

Waiting in their hotel room, the two of the Foundation watched the missing manic selling chewing gum on TV. High as kites, they primed themselves for the raid tonight. The drugs were secure but the money was still needed.

"What time is it?"

"It's late."

"We'll go."

"Yes."

Quietly igniting the engine of their rented BMW, they drove back to Jeeves' studio. Both clad in black, they pulled up outside, opposite, waited for a definite all-clear, before Jeremy slipped out the passenger seat, strolled around the rear and clambered onto the tatty fire escape. He climbed up the black, metal steps, taking care to keep the volume down, stealthily reaching the top and the window to Jeeves' office. Blessed with a cat burglar's skill, silently he jemmied the window, emitting only a slight screech as he pushed it open and pounced inside. In the darkness, he hopped over the sill, landed squarely on his feet and flicked on his torch. The safe was exposed, in the framework and with a life-time's experience behind him, Jeremy cracked the combination, his deft fingering easily negotiating the lock and the code. After five minutes or so and with silent breath, he swung the metal door open, shone the torch in, spied the money, grabbed the lot and placed it in his bag. Quickly, he zipped it up and then paused as he heard noises coming from the landing. He stopped, looked and listened again, heard a low murmur and footsteps on the stairs and flew out the window.

# 5

Landing on the metal grille of the firescape, his slim feet sent shudders, shuddering through the metal grille, just as the studio burst open, lights were turned on and shouts were heard. Scrambling, Jeremy hopped down the steps, two by two. Above him, someone clambered out the window, tripped and fell loudly and dropped his torch,that smashed on the ground as Jeremy reached halfway. Now, jumping on the escape, pounding on the grill-like grille, he reached the snowy sidewalk, ran past rows of baroque statues of men saluting and women looking confused, before stopping sharply, spinning around and wondering where the fuck Nigel was.

Along back alleys and rear avenues, headlights dipped and glowed in a metallic game of cat and mouse. The beautiful dutch air, keeping noise to a minimum, cut out the excess of the engines and Jeremy tapped his foot impatiently.

Commotion behind him lent urgency and he ran ahead, tightly clutching the strap of the bag. He ducked in a crevice, popped out again, cursed the missing Nige and double-backed on himself, skirting down a side-street, running out into the open air and lashing into a busy street. In a flow of vehicles, the lights of the BMW came out of the night, the insufferably cool Nigel behind the wheel. He pulled up, opened the passenger door and took off again with Jeremy half-in, legs hanging out.

"Motherfuckers."

They sped along an angled Interhuizen street.

"Look, look. Motherfuckers."

Jeremy twisted his head. From out of the darkness was the competition, obviously wise (probably tipped off by the conniving Jeeves), gaining ground behind them as Nigel K navigated the system. He took a sharp left, a BMW hubcap flying off the wheel in a steely circular motion across the road and kneecapping a pedestrian.

The genius of the Dutch planners had laid the streets out straight. Nigel revving the motor for all it was worth, only a little bit self-conscious of the disturbance he was creating, the messy squall of the exhaust disrupting the heavenly static of the marijuana air.

Passers-by stopped, watched, waved, as first the BMW flew past, closely followed by an Audi and a Merc. One blue, one red, desperately gaining on the grey saloon in front, zig-zagging through the town.

At traffic lights, they broke them all, a multitude of vans and motors spinning, braking, squealing and screeching as Nigel flung a right, taking a kerb, pulling the car on the pavement and driving through a random set-up of cardboard boxes. Reaching the end of yet another sparkling street, he took another left, into a late-night market-place, the Audi following and the Merc yanking on an alternative route. Through fruit stalls and vegetable shops, the BMW drove through them all, throwing a hail of tomatoes and celery into the sky in a multi-coloured rainbow of natural goodness. Stalls fell over, the tented roofs crashing to the ground, the unfortunate traders diving for cover as the race continued.

# 6

Now, sexily unrepentant at the havoc being caused by the speeding chase, Nigel powered on, clicking on the pedal and making ground. Round a roundabout, he drove, the Merc appearing again from the right and the Audi driving over the circle.

"Where are the cops?" muttered Jeremy, as another innocent car spun off the road.

In a three-pronged attack, the cars reaching ninety, the traffic slowed and dispersed, the BMW out front, knocking Renaults and Fiestas out of the way, until an obstinate wanker in a jeep refused to move over, locking doors on the passenger side, sparking sparks, the wanker gesticulating wildly out the window in a faggot motion to the arrogant Jeremy. Nigel, showing divine strength, lurched the BMW to the right, swung back violently, bashed the jeep, not once but twice, until the driver lost control, went up a grassy verge, crashed off-road and blew-up in flames.

It was right about then, that the mustachioed passenger of the Merc behind, lent out the side window and began firing shots at the BMW. A bullet pinged off the brake-light, smashing glass, but missing the tyres. Nigel squealed ahead, the cars now leaving the town, but joined by the sirens of a passing police car. In the tranquil countryside, calm and still, the diamond of cars sped along, until the blue Merc and the red Audi, driven in parallel fashion, overshot their limits, one crashing into the other, the two of them together, flipping and rolling, coming to rest in a mangled mess of wreckage and rubble, the occupants laboriously struggling out, only to be stopped by the guns of the coppers who banged them up against their cars and nicked the lot of them.

"Thank heavens for the Dutch polis," said Jeremy, skinning a joint on the door of the glove compartment.

"We have succeeded. Yes?"

"Yes!" and the two drove into the night loaded with cash and free drugs.

Back at the university, Melissa and Lieza, were saying their goodbyes to the faculty staff. To all their tutors, good and bad, before packing their bags and preparing to go. Jeremy had tipped them off about his safety net plan, knowing the weather can be better elsewhere.

They took one last trip along the campus, waving farewell to old friends and new, and saying a fond adieu to the soulful guys of the communist branch, before stumbling across the bumbling Terrence, the tag 'WARD SECURITY' proudly emblazoned upon his chest. He wished them well and they went their way. Terrence, growing tired, patrolled back to his office; he and Vaughan were just starting a shift, through to the next morning and they settled in for a languid smoking session, before preparing for a few hours paid sleep.

Before that though, Terrence arranged the cameras in the following formation:

(Formula and sequence available to the highest bidder)★

After a peaceful night of doing nothing and damning consistency to hell, Terrence strolled home, got in the front door, turned on the telly, kicked off his shoes, put up his feet and switched on CNBC...

8

...and so, S awoke from his Norwegian dream – and don't worry, you'll know it when it happens – to the smooth sounds of the sweet and soulful archangel Gabriel Hannon; fresh back from Holland, dressed all in black, to start another day. The cash had been split, Nigel disappearing with his half, Jeremy waiting for Melissa to arrive. Waiting patiently, he smoked casually, pondering where they should live. At 11.00, Melissa arrived. He gave her the bag for safe-keeping and arranged to meet her later. He walked into town, purchased two plane tickets to Amsterdam, some new shoes and an Irish passport under the name of Luke O'Doherty. Later still, he waited with a suit of luggage, sitting on a bench, hoping no-one spotted him.

Half an hour after the arranged time, Melissa turned up in a Volkswagon, driven by Lieza. She stepped out the passenger side.

"I got the tickets," he said.

He walked over to her, she handed him the bag, kissed him on the mouth and said "I gotta go." She got back in the beetle and Lieza took off with a cheeky backwave, leaving Jeremy standing by the bench. He lent down and opened the zip. Inside the hold-all was a note that read:

> You don't love me. I don't mind
> What would it be like in 26,000 years time.

He looked further down in the hold-all and half the money was gone. He slumped back onto the bench and put his head down, between his legs, thinking things over, when suddenly he heard a voice.

Everybody listen to the hill... said the voice... yet when he turned around no-one was there. Looking back and wondering why, a new light dawned awake, and it was then that he remembered that it was NOAH, the backward God, that led all the animals in, 2 x 2...

# 9

Arup was playing with his testicles, marvelling at their elasticity when Andrews barged in.

"Mister Arup, sir, we have a problem. It appears as if Jeremy S and Nigel K have taken off with the drugs and the money from the Interhuizen deal."

Arup exploded. "What?! This is preposterous. How could this happen?! Tell me Andrews, how did you let this happen?"

Andrews was silent.

"I demand an answer, Andrews, how did this happen? Tell me now!"

Andrews stuttered, "Um, well... it appears as if we trusted them too much, sir."

"Andrews," screamed Arup, "you are a biscuit! Get out!"

Andrews shuffled out and Arup fumed, his eyes bulging out of his face. "As if, as if... as if this wasn't enough. I pay these people well. I ask for little in return, humble as I am, I could fund a nation, I could feed a world. I should be a saviour, a prophet, but shame upon shame, my own people rip me off, tear me apart and damage my soul. I show them the future and give them the scientific degree, no matter what pain in my belly.

I suffer for all... and for what, for WHAT? And to finish it all, to mock and to taunt, to haunt me further, I bring forth life, this creature, this beast, the spawn of Satan, this... this thing, this alien, but to cap it all, to clear me out, I realize now, looking back, I understand now... the fucking alien is bent."

Arup lifted his leg and burped and farted simultaneously...

# 10

... And what of Jesus, I hear you ask, the dead dude with a beard who once stepped in a puddle, yeah, well, maybe we can name the global watch after him... the Joseph Conrad clock or something like that. Anyway it was all academic to Simpson; Jeremy, now, sitting as he was on the balcony of a Parisienne bistro, just watching the world stroll by and waiting for his time to come round. Time enough to entertain himself with the entire collected, literary works and musical accomplishments of the great J. G. Ballard, before exploring the investigation of the joint Dutch-Russian space programme and the possibility of the Shakespeare collective.

Whatever, one thing was for sure... now, it was open season, a free-for-all, with the only catch being... it's got to be done with style!